Harder than the Rest
MacLarens of Fire Mountain

SHIRLEEN DAVIES

Book Three in the MacLarens of Fire Mountain
Series

For permission requests, contact the publisher.

Avalanche Ranch Press, LLC
PO Box 12618
Prescott, AZ 86304

Harder than the Rest is a work of fiction. Names, characters, places and incidents are either products of the author's imagination or used factiously. Any resemblance to actual events, locales, or persons, living or dead, is wholly coincidental.

ISBN-10: 098967732X
ISBN-13: 978-0-9896773-2-5
Library of Congress Control Number: 2013919108

Cover artwork by idrewdesign.

Description

"They are men you want on your side. Hard, confident, and loyal, the MacLarens of Fire Mountain will seize your attention from the first page."

Will MacLaren is a hardened, plain-speaking bounty hunter. His life centers on finding men guilty of horrendous crimes and making sure justice is done. There is no place in his world for the carefree attitude he carried years before when a tragic event destroyed his dreams.

Amanda is the daughter of a successful Colorado rancher. Determined and proud, she works hard to prove she is as capable as any man and worthy to be her father's heir. When a stranger arrives, her independent nature collides with the strong pull toward the handsome ranch hand. But is he what he seems and could his secrets endanger her as well as her family?

The last thing Will needs is to feel passion for another woman. But Amanda elicits feelings he thought were long buried. Can Will's desire for her change him? Or will the vengeance he seeks against the one man he wants to destroy—a dangerous opponent without a conscious—continue to control his life?

Dedication

This book is dedicated to our three oldest sons, Justin, Brandon, and Martin. Each is special in their own, unique way, and each has brought meaning to the terms dedication, family, and loyalty. I love you all.

Acknowledgements

As with the first two books in this series, I want to thank my editor, Regge Episale, who continues to be a beacon through my writing journey.

Thanks also to my beta readers, including my wonderful husband, Richard. Their input and suggestions are insightful and greatly appreciated.

Finally, many thanks to my wonderful resources, including Diane Lebow, who has been a whiz at guiding my social media endeavors.

Harder

than the Rest

Harder than the Rest

Prologue

New Mexico Territory, 1886

"Don't shoot, MacLaren. I'm laid-up, can't hurt you none." The old man pleaded from his bunk in the dirty hidden shack. He'd been holed-up for a couple of weeks, with little food and less water, since taking a shot in the leg during a robbery that had gone wrong. He'd barely escaped alive. His sons hadn't been so fortunate.

"You hear me? I ain't no threat to you." He shifted his weight on the old mattress, trying to get a better view of the man standing just outside the door.

No answer came. The old man could just see the silhouette of the bounty hunter who'd tracked him. MacLaren wasn't human, at least that's what others said of him, and the old man had joined the ranks of believers.

No one knew of this old shack where he and his boys hid after each robbery. It lay tucked deep into the rugged mountains north of Splitshot, New Mexico, and took several days on horseback to reach. He guessed no one had ever tracked them closer than ten miles. All had given up and turned back. All except Will MacLaren.

"Hear me good, old man. Makes no difference to me if I take you in alive or dead. Full of holes or not, I know you can walk, cause I've been watching." MacLaren shifted his stance from his location behind a tree, about ten feet from the cabin entrance. "And I'd think twice about trying to run if I were you. If you do, you'll be dead before you get five feet." His voice was hard, rough, and raspy, the result of an ambush several years before. There was no mistaking that he meant what he said.

"Now, you know I ain't able to run like you're thinking, MacLaren." He changed positions once more to adjust the blanket that covered his legs. "I'd have a better chance with a judge than with you."

"If that's what you think, then you'd best give up and come on out. I'll make sure you get your trial. No one has to die here today." Will continued to glance around the brush and trees that encircled the house. He was confident the old man was alone, but being careless had cost him in the past, and he had no intention of ever being taken by surprise again. "Let's not waste anymore time, Tankard. Come out or I'll come in and get you."

"Now, I ain't so sure I'd make it back alive. Way I hear it, you bring just as many back wrapped in a blanket."

Will knew the old man was stalling but he couldn't detect any movement from his current position. He shifted a few inches as he gazed into the dark cabin, and saw it—shiny metal that poked out from the blanket's edge. His hand gripped tighter on his own rifle. He brought the gun up to his shoulder. "I'm saying it once more. Don't do anything stupid. There's just no chance you'll make it through this alive if you do."

But as the last words were said, Tankard pulled a gun from under the blanket and tried to get a shot off before MacLaren had time to react. It wasn't to be.

Two seconds later the old man lay dead. As far as MacLaren was concerned, Tankard and both his sons, Billy and Tuck, could rot in hell together. Jamie, Will's older brother, should've killed Billy when he had the chance several years ago, but as a U.S. Marshal he'd done what was expected, what was right, and arrested him instead. Will didn't know how many other people had died at Billy's hand since then, but there would be no more. Their reign of robbing and killing had ended.

Within the hour Will MacLaren, with Tankard's body wrapped in a blanket and secured to the old man's horse, began the long trek down the mountain.

Chapter One

Splitshot was a growing community located in what many considered to be a desolate area in the Northern New Mexico Territory, with little water and less commerce. Will told himself that he had come here because of the reward on the Tankard family, but he'd fought his way up the mountains through the rough terrain, changing weather, and sudden hazards because he knew what kind of animal he tracked. Old man Tankard was a heartless, cold-blooded murderer, with no reluctance about killing an innocent man, woman, or child, if they stood in the way of what he wanted. Human life meant nothing to him and had meant little more to either of his sons. But they were no longer a concern to law-abiding people, like his family back home in Fire Mountain, Arizona Territory. Tonight the bounty hunter would celebrate a righteous death.

"MacLaren. Buy you a drink?" Sheriff Cordell McAllister grabbed a chair and sat down at Will's table without invitation. He knew he didn't need one. Cordell had known Will since they'd sat next to each other at the schoolhouse in Fire Mountain. They'd become best friends. The two of them, plus Will's twin brother, Drew, had shared so many adventures that they'd never be able to remember them all.

"Anytime, Cord," Will said without looking up from the whiskey he nursed.

"Slow night," Cord added idly. He held up his drink and pointed it around the almost empty saloon. "Tomorrow will be different, being Saturday night and all. Then the locals will come in, have a few drinks, turn into idiots, and make my life exciting." He smiled and downed the whiskey in one gulp.

"Exciting?" Will looked up at his friend.

"Well, you know my life isn't as interesting as yours—traveling around, finding the bad boys, making great money. I'm just a small town sheriff. I have to find excitement where I can."

Will just shook his head and continued to study his whiskey. It had been a long few weeks. He'd rest up a spell then find another job that would take him away from Splitshot, possibly out of New Mexico. It had been a long time since he'd been around people who'd known him before his life had changed. Each job seemed to take him further and further away from his roots and the few people he still felt comfortable with. Cord was one of those people. He wished he could stay longer, soak up the warmth and kindness his friend offered, but he knew the past would intrude. It always did.

"What are your plans, Will? Aren't you ready to give this up? Go home?" The concern in Cord's voice was not lost on Will. The compassion was well intended, but Will just didn't want to be dragged into that conversation again.

"Not yet, Cord. Don't know when I'll be ready. Maybe never."

"It's been over five years. You've spent the whole time going after the types of men who did this to you, to Emily. We all loved her, Will, but you've got to move on. Live the life you were supposed to live."

"Yea, Cord, and what life is that?" Will knew his already rough voice was strained, edgy, but he hated talking about that fateful morning, years before, and the losses he'd suffered.

"Ranching, breeding horses, all the stuff you planned to do before she died," Cord replied quietly, not wanting to set Will off, but needing to get his point across.

"Those plans are as dead as Emily. They mean nothing to me without her." He swallowed the amber liquid in his glass and poured another. "You know that we'd just finished the house. Baby was due in about four months. Emily had just started feeling better," Will said, more to himself than to Cord. Cord had heard the story many times, but always let his friend talk it out. "Shouldn't have let her convince me to take her off the ranch. If I'd followed my gut and stood firm..." his agonized voice trailed off.

"Wasn't your fault, none of it." Cord struggled to find the right words, but in five years he'd never come up with them. Didn't figure he would tonight. "The filly you wanted for Emily was available and she insisted on going with you. I doubt anyone could've kept her at the ranch. How were you to know the Hawley's would break Chad out of jail and head directly across your path? You've blamed yourself for all these years and there's just no sense to it anymore."

Will sat quiet for so long that Cord didn't think he'd answer. "Doesn't matter. She's gone, along with our baby. You know, Cord, she was the only woman I ever wanted. I'm not interested in another, not to love anyway. My life is fine as it is."

Leaning forward and placing his arms on the table, Cord looked square into Will's haunted eyes. "Do you think that's what Emily would want for you? Becoming a hired gun, never settling down? Do you think she could love the man you're becoming?" He could see Will's face harden and back straighten at the words, but continued. "You got them, all of them. Buried Emily, tracked the Hawley's down and brought them in for the justice they deserved—well, at least the two you didn't kill, and the one we heard got shot dead near Santa Fe. He was the last. It's time to go home before this type of life consumes you and you won't be able to stop. That's all I'm saying."

Will shot back the whiskey and slammed his glass on the table before standing to stare down at a man he loved like a brother. "Everything you say is true. I know it. But it doesn't make a bit of difference to me. I know you mean well, but it's my problem. That life's over. The man you knew is long gone."

"So you're just giving up. Going to continue this until someone kills you and ends your misery?" Cord couldn't believe this was the same joking, carefree Will of their youth—the relaxed boy who'd displayed a constant smile and pulled endless pranks—the man everyone could count on to be the first to offer help or just an ear, and who could joke anyone out of a sour mood.

"That's exactly what I'm saying," Will replied truthfully. "Go home to June and your kids. Tell them goodbye for me." He walked to the door before turning and adding, almost as an afterthought. "Take care, Cord."

******

Fire Mountain, Arizona Territory

"Any word, Tom?" Jamie MacLaren walked into the telegraph office with his young son, Isaac, following at a slow pace, looking up at the tall counter and the thin man smiling down at him.

"Jamie, how you doing today?" Tom had known the MacLaren family for years, watched the brothers grow up. And like many in Fire Mountain, he knew of their accomplishments, failures, and struggles.

"Good, Tom. Real good. Looking for news from either of our errant brothers. Got anything for me?" Jamie reached down to pick up his son and position him on top of the counter.

"A message from Drew just came in," Tom said as he reached over to grab the telegraph and hand it to Jamie. "Nothing from Will. Any idea where he is right how?"

"Nothing since the last message a couple of months ago from Cord McAllister saying he was in Splitshot, looking for old man Tankard. It's killing Aunt Alicia to not know what goes on with that kid." He moved a squirming Isaac from the counter and placed him back on the wood floor. "Niall's about ready to ride out to New Mexico and

14

track him down, and if he goes, I just may go with him." The disgusted look, and tone of Jamie's voice, illustrated the frustration all the MacLarens felt at the lack of communication from Will.

"It's a hard thing, loosing family. Especially someone like Emily. Each man deals with it in his own time. Can't force 'em to do it any other way. At least that's the way I look at it," Tom said, his voice full of sympathy.

Jamie couldn't remember anyone other than Tom ever running the telegraph office. Besides Reverend Blanchard, Tom probably knew more about the people of the town than anyone else. And he was a good friend.

"Yea, I know you're right, but it's hard on the family. We just wish he'd put this quest for revenge, or justice, as he calls it, behind him. Come home." Jamie read the message from the other twin, Drew, laughed softly, then folded it and tucked it into his shirt pocket. "Well, we'd best get going. Got a supply list a yard long today. Thanks." Jamie shook Tom's hand, picked up Isaac, and left to deliver Drew's message and lack of news from Will to Aunt Alicia.

Chapter Two

Cold Creek, Colorado

"Ah, come on, Amanda. How long can dinner take? There's still plenty of light left. I'll even ride with you, if you like." Chet smiled at the young woman he'd been pursuing for several months. She was a tough one all right.

"Stop, Chet." Amanda held up her hand as if to ward off the man blocking her path. "I've told you I'm not interested in having dinner with you." Amanda's exasperation showed. The cowboy had become too pushy, almost insulting in his advances. "I don't have time for dinner. I need to get back to the ranch and Joey." She looked over her shoulder. "See, there's Jake now." She pointed to a man on horseback coming up behind Chet.

The older man rode up next to her. "You all set, Amanda?"

"Sure am, Jake." Amanda smiled as he helped steady her horse, Angel, so she could mount. "Let's get going."

"Some day you'll change your mind, Amanda, and I'll be waiting," Chet yelled after her. She turned her horse in the direction of the ranch.

"What was that all about?" Jake asked once they were outside of Cold Creek, the town closest to the ranch.

"Nothing. He's just a nuisance, nothing more." Amanda refused to dwell on Chet or his persistent requests to court her. She had much more important things on her mind. "So what did Whitaker say about selling us the bull?" She'd been negotiating for this particular animal for months, and Whitaker finally seemed interested.

"I think we're breaking through to him." Jake sounded pleased that they might be one step closer to buying the bull that could produce the kind of stock needed in this mountainous and cold region of Colorado. "We started talking price and I don't think we're that far off. Told him I'd check with him again in a few days. Got to head back into Cold Creek anyway to pick up the supplies we ordered. Maybe I'll return with a bull, too."

"That's good, but just don't let him push you over our limit. I only have so much to put towards this bull." Although the ranch did well, cash was always tight. Her father had established a line of credit before he and her mother had left for their long-awaited trip to Europe, but Amanda didn't want to use it unless she had to.

"Look, Amanda, I already told you that Grant would want you to use the credit he setup for the ranch." Jake held up his hand when Amanda started to respond. "Now hear me out. You know this bull is critical to improving the herd. You know your Pa would approve. Right now there are at least two other ranchers who want that bull. The one who gets it is going to be in real good shape. The ones who don't, well, they'll have a long ways to catch up. This is a prize animal and there just isn't another like him, not in these parts, anyway.

We don't want them to know we're close to getting it. May start a bidding war. Let's just pay the price and move the bull over to the Big G."

"There's only one man that would cause problems and try to outbid us, but he's got other issues with my father and me, and you know it. The others don't have the funds. Most have been very supportive of my father's wishes for me to learn the business. Gordon's the only one that seems to be against the idea, and he's been running out of steam lately. Maybe his new wife, Eloise, is having a positive impact on him after all." Amanda guided Angel over the steep terrain that signaled the entrance to the Taylor ranch, the Big G.

"Maybe so, but that don't mean he won't try to grab that bull out from under us if he gets wind that we're close. Any advantage, such as a prime animal like that one, gives a rancher an edge. There's been bad blood between Gordon Bierdan and your father for as long as I can remember, and Gordon's always wanted the Big G. Never figured why he thought your Pa would sell. It's common knowledge that Grant plans to pass the ranch on to you someday. But, when that day comes, I think Gordon will do whatever it takes to get it from you." Jake followed Amanda down the steep slope. They could've taken the easier path through the valley, but it would've taken longer, and Amanda was anxious to get back to her ten-year-old brother, Joey.

"I know you're right," Amanda conceded. "For now, let's focus on bringing that bull home. Pay what you have to and I'll draw from the bank if needed." She liked Jake and respected him a great deal. He was her father's foreman and had been a fixture at the ranch since before Amanda was born. All the ranchers respected him, which proved to be a great benefit to someone like Amanda, who'd spent the last few years in school back East. Jake had to be over fifty, but her father had said more than once that he'd hate to go up against him in a fight. She understood.

******

Splitshot, New Mexico

Will sat in his room at the boarding house, looking at an old, faded poster of the man he would go after next. Groups were his preference—two, three, four—didn't matter, he just preferred going after more men to spending his time on only one. But this one was different. This was the one he needed to get. Maybe then he could put the past behind him, at last.

Emily. His heart always twisted when he thought of his wife and their unborn child. How different his life would have been if she were still here.

He sank deeper into the bed, rested his arm over his eyes, and thought of that one horrific day that had driven him across three territories, a couple of states, and might eventually lead him to hell.

Five years earlier, Fire Mountain, Arizona

"Will, you're talking crazy. No one names a boy Apollo or a girl Aphrodite. Can you imagine the teasing from other children? Not to mention what your brothers would say to those names. Nope. There is no chance you get to the name the baby." Emily had grown used to Will's humor. He'd always been the one to liven things up and tease her into laughing. Of all the MacLarens, he could be counted on to find the absurdity in a bad situation.

She sat back against the hard seat of the wagon as they continued on the rutty road to the neighbor's ranch. The MacLaren's wanted a foal from Ed Williamson's mare to strengthen their breeding program. He'd agreed to sell them the next little filly the mare produced, and now they were heading over to view it. Wouldn't be ready to bring back for a while, but Emily couldn't wait that long. Truthfully, neither could Will.

"Well then, how about we name the filly Aphrodite, or maybe Athena? Both are great names." Will tried to straighten his long legs and adjusted in his seat. He'd much rather they were on horses, but there wasn't a chance he'd let Emily ride at this point in her pregnancy.

Emily held her hat down with one hand and peered over at her husband as the names rolled around in her mind. "Athena? Well, that may be a good name for the filly. Has a certain ring and there sure isn't anyone else who'd use it." She smiled. "Guess we'll just have to see her before we make a decision." Emily beamed at the thought of the filly and the fun she'd have training her. Athena might, indeed, be an appropriate name for the very special animal that was destined to improve their breeding program. Emily looked ahead at the bend in the trail that would take them past a pine forest. They would start the descent to the valley below soon, and on toward the Williamson's ranch. Not long now.

It all happened in seconds. One minute they were laughing, joking about baby names, and the next they were surrounded by six men, all with guns pointed at them. Too late, Will tried to reach for his pistol. One of the men got off a shot that hit Will in the shoulder, while another man produced a whip and slashed it around Will's neck, pulling him backwards into the bed of the buckboard. The whip tightened so he couldn't breathe, and yanked him to the ground below. Will tried to work his fingers between the leather and his neck.

Emily screamed, called his name. Her voice— strident and insulting—abraded the man who had shot her husband. Will fought unconsciousness. His fingers tore at the whip around his neck. His lungs burned. He called to her, but no sound emerged. Will tried, one last time, to lift his head. The whip jerked again, dragged him through the dirt, further from the buckboard. His mind screamed his wife's name. He grabbed wildly for anyone, anything, but caught only air. Will fought. Emily's screams faded and died. His struggles slowed. He lost the fight. His mind closed and darkness took over.

******

Will didn't know how long he'd been out. When he came to, it was dark. He shivered in the cold, damp air. He could hear men's voices. *Where am I?* It started coming back to him. Men, guns, Emily. *Emily! God, where is Emily?* He tried to sit up but a firm hand pushed him back down.

"Found him, Ed. Over here. Bring a blanket and water. Will's been shot and it don't look good."

Will tried to sit up, but again was pushed back to the ground. Hands gently probed the wounds on his shoulder and neck. Someone placed a blanket over him to stifle the chills.

"Emily?" He tried to speak but all that came out were raspy sounds that even he couldn't understand. His throat was on fire. He found it hard to get his breath.

"God, son, what did those bastards do to you?" Ed said to himself more than anyone else. "Jim, we need to stop the bleeding and get a doc quick. Let's load him into the buckboard. I'll head to the ranch, see what we can do for him while you go for Doc McCauley."

"Ed," Jim spoke in a soft voice so that Will wouldn't hear. "What about Emily? We can't just leave her. Critters could get to her before we get back."

"Yea, I know. Once Will is settled in the buckboard, we'll wrap her up and place her in back with him. There isn't anything else to do. He's going to find out soon enough anyway. With his throat the way it is, we can't even get him liquored up to help dull the pain." Ed swore as he looked at the bloody form of his old friend's nephew and thought of Emily, and the baby no one would ever know.

Mercifully, Will passed out while they settled him into the wagon and didn't wake during the trip to the house or when Ed called for help to carry him inside. They did all they could. The bullet to his shoulder had hit high on his right side and passed clean through. The wound to his neck caused the most concern.

"Where is he?" Ed could here the doctor, Caleb McCauley, shout as he came into the house.

"Back here, doc, in my office. Didn't want to risk getting him upstairs. He's hurt bad. Hope you can help him." Ed looked down at the young man and prayed he'd make it.

Caleb didn't reply, just rolled up his sleeves, walked to the kitchen to wash his hands, then returned to focus on his friend. He'd known Will for several years, since a stagecoach accident had injured Caleb and his traveling companions. They were all brought to Fire Mountain, and all had stayed. Sam Browning became a deputy sheriff, Kate Garner married Will's brother, Niall, and Caleb took over the medical practice of the town's long-time physician, Doc Minton.

Will drifted in and out of consciousness. The doc made quick work of his shoulder wound, then began to focus on the more difficult throat damage. The whip had cut deep into his neck, damaged several layers of skin, and penetrated the muscles around his throat. By all rights Will should be dead from what those bastards had done, but somehow he had survived. Caleb wondered if Will would care once he learned of Emily and their unborn child.

******

It should be me in that box, Will thought as they gently lowered Emily into her grave. Doc McCauley told him he wasn't recovered enough to attend, but the doc knew his friend wouldn't listen. As he suspected, Will refused to stay behind. He would be there for her, and their baby. He couldn't save them, but he wouldn't be denied saying goodbye.

John and Marie Ellen Jacobson, Emily's parents, stood on his right while his brothers stood on his left. Even Drew had taken time from his legal studies to come home and support his twin brother. All four brothers together. It had been rare the last few years, but the senseless violence that had cost them Emily had also reunited them.

Ed had sent for Will's oldest brother, Niall, and other brother, Jamie, the night of the attack. They had arrived within a few hours and found Will upstairs, swearing in an almost unintelligible rasping voice, demanding answers. Wanting Emily.

He'd gone crazy when Niall had told him about the tragedy.

"She was beaten, Will. Badly from the looks of it." Niall words were soft and pained, but his voice was firm. "Her clothing was torn. Doc McCauley believes she was strangled to stop her from screaming, while they...huh..." he paused to take a shaky breath, but couldn't continue.

The recognition on Will's face was instantaneous.

It had taken both brothers, plus Ed, to hold Will down while Caleb administered laudanum. After the effects wore off, he didn't react at all, and refused anything that might dull the pain. He wanted to feel it—yearned to do whatever he could to allow the agony he felt to continue. He deserved no less. Even his twin brother, Drew, who was closer to him than anyone else, had been pushed away. Will wanted no comfort, no excuses, no words from anyone saying it wasn't his fault. In his heart, he knew they were wrong. In his heart, he'd already accepted that he was responsible for their deaths.

Two days passed without further response from Will, worrying everyone, but no one more than his Aunt Alicia. She, with her late husband Stuart, had raised all four boys when their parents were killed years before. She couldn't have loved them more if they'd been her own sons. Their love for her was just as strong.

Alicia stayed next to him at the grave site when the service was over. "Would you like us to stay awhile?"

Will continued to stand, staring at the open grave. He didn't answer her.

Niall walked up and laid a hand on his brother's shoulder. Will shrugged it off and continued to stare into the nothingness in front of him. From where he stood, his life was now just an open void without meaning or direction. How could they understand the dark despair he felt, or the guilt?

Chapter Three

Will woke with a start as the sound of gunfire penetrated his brain. A dream. He'd had another dream. Sweat beaded on his forehead and he swiped at the dampness with his hand. The gunfire started again. What the hell was happening? Reaching for his gun belt, he jumped from the bed to look out the window above the street. Nothing for a moment, then another shot rang through the early morning air.

Will threw on his pants, boots, and shirt, strapped on the Colt, grabbed his rifle, and took the stairs at a run. He paused outside the hotel and listened again. It sounded like the shots were coming from down by the jail.

"Let him out, Cord. You know you can't hold him for killing that drifter," a man yelled. "There're plenty who'll say he pulled his gun on my boy first. It was self-defense, pure and simple."

When the sheriff didn't respond, the man and his two companions started to pepper the jail with more bullets.

"That's enough, gentlemen." A strong, hard voice came from behind the three men. Turning as one, they saw a lone man behind them with a rifle leveled at the one who had been yelling for Cord. "I'm sure the Sheriff will be happy to speak with you if you lay down your guns and walk in peaceably."

"This is none of your business, stranger. This is between us and the Sheriff."

"Maybe so, but anyone shooting up the jail like that is either asking for a bullet or too stupid to understand the trouble he's stirring up." Will's voice didn't waiver, and he focused even more firmly on the one man who seemed to be the leader. "Now, throw your guns down and we'll all go inside so this matter can be cleared up."

The man's face turned dark red at the obvious insult.

"There's three of us, mister. You'll be dead by one of us. Can't kill us all."

"That might be true, but you'll go with me, unless you talk your friends into laying down their guns. Now." Will was out of patience.

The man seemed to think it over a minute before responding. "Lay down your guns, boys," he said through gritted teeth. "We'll go in and talk to Cord, like the stranger here says. Then we'll take Harley home."

The others dropped their guns and dismounted to join their leader near the door of the jail. Will kept a close eye on all three, his gun never wavering.

"Cord? It's Will. I'm coming in with these three ingrates. Don't shoot."

The sheriff opened the door, gun in hand, and motioned them all inside.

"Take a seat, Floyd, and tell me what you want." Cord's voice was affable, but Will recognized the steel behind the words. He followed the men through the door and leaned against the doorjamb, gun ready, as the others found chairs or leaned against a wall.

"We came for Harley. You can't arrest him for protecting himself from that drifter. We got witnesses who'll back us up." Floyd Bell glared at the sheriff.

"That so? And just who would those witnesses be?" Cord clearly didn't believe the man.

"Well, Fred Stone, for one, and Davey Stewart for another." Bell didn't like being questioned, especially by a low-paid lawman. Hell, he was a prosperous rancher, part of the town council that had hired McAllister, and made at least ten times what the sheriff made.

"Can't see how that can be, Floyd. Fred and Davey got rowdy early. Had to put them in cells to sleep it off. Let them out late last night when I brought Harley in. Couldn't stand the noise with all three shouting." Cord knew Floyd wouldn't leave without Harley, and wouldn't hesitate to exert his power with the town leaders to get his son released.

The room fell silent.

"You listen to me, Cord. I helped hire you and I can see that you're run out of Splitshot just as quick. We thought you understood the rules when you took the badge, but appears not. Some things, Sheriff, are just, shall we say, ignored, if you get my meaning." The rancher's voice had risen along with the color in his already ruddy complexion.

"Do what you think you must, Floyd. Harley killed a man last night and I have three witnesses that saw the whole thing. To a man, they stated Harley drew first after he couldn't shame the man into pulling his gun. Best thing you could do for your son is get a good lawyer, because believe me, he's going to need one." Cord paused to confirm there was no confusion on his stance. "By the way, did I mention that I'm one of the witnesses?"

Floyd's fist slammed down on the sheriff's desk. "Damn you, Cord. You're making a big mistake forcing this. I'll be back with an order from the judge to release him, and Harley better be in good shape when I return." He motioned to the other two to head out. Floyd shoved past Will, knocking him into the jamb in his rush to leave the jail behind.

"I'd say that went well," Cord snorted, pulling out his chair to sit and motioning for Will to do the same.

"Who are they?"

"Floyd Bell, his son, Carl, and one of his hands. Other son is Harley, locked up in back. Bell thinks he owns this town, but most others don't agree and would like nothing better than to see him taken down a bit."

"Harley guilty?"

"As they get. He'll probably hang for this one, unless his Pa manages to buy-off the judge and intimidate a few others. They're a rotten group, Will. Too bad, cause the town has a lot of real good people." Cord sighed as he leaned back in his chair, entwining his hands behind his head and closing his eyes.

"Why do you stay?" Will had never understood why Cord stayed in the small town. Although the trees and elevation could be majestic, a showplace it wasn't. "You could move back to Fire Mountain.

Hell, Niall would hire you right off, and probably any number of others."

"Been thinking about that. June's from here. Her parents still lived in Splitshot when we married. Now that they're gone, no real reason to stay. You know my family's still in Fire Mountain, and Pa's not getting any better. Ma writes that his back is getting worse every day and he tires easily. Got a message from the Deputy Sheriff, Sam Browning, that Sheriff Joe Rawlins is retiring. Can you imagine? He's finally giving it up. Anyway, Joe wants Sam to take over as Sheriff. Sam's asked me if I'm interested in being his deputy." Cord smiled at the thought of heading back to Arizona and continuing as a sheriff. "Yep, going home sounds better all the time, and we may just do it. You could come with us, Will." Cord sat up and folded his hands on the desk. "Might even let you boss me around if I decided not to work with Sam and went to work at your place instead. Great opportunity for you to get back at me." His smile widened. Cord hoped his friend would at least consider it.

"You just don't give up," Will responded quietly. He could tell by the look in Cord's face that he, June, and the kids would be leaving for Fire Mountain soon. He was a good sheriff and would jump at the chance to work with Sam. Cord would never be happy working at the ranch, but a position as deputy sheriff was a whole different situation.

"No reason to. Now, get out of here and let me do my job. Come by the house for supper tonight, and don't tell me you're leaving today because

June would skin us both if you left without saying goodbye to her and the kids."

******

It had rained for three days without letting up. Slow, but persistent, which kept his clothes and horse soaked. The wind had died down so at least the chill seemed tolerable. He could feel the temperatures dropping. Snow could come at any time and Will had no desire to get caught outside of Cold Creek, Colorado when the first storm hit.

The last word MacLaren had received confirmed that a man named Chet Hollis had been living in Cold Creek for a few years. The informant didn't believe Hollis to be the man Will hunted. Nonetheless, Will had a sense about such things, and there were just too many similarities to ignore. The reward was good, and if this turned out to be his man, it would be worth riding halfway up Western Colorado to the small cattle town on the Gundy River.

He'd had to battle both June and Cord the night before he left. They'd made the decision to return home to Fire Mountain and were determined to talk him into going back with them, but he'd held firm. Whether they accepted his new life or not, he had become someone that even he couldn't have imagined before Emily's death. A bounty hunter, bringing in fugitives that regular lawmen couldn't find, and staying around to make sure that justice prevailed. He'd refused all help from his ex-marshal-brother, Jamie, and his oldest brother, Niall's, father-in-law, Trent Garner, who had retired from the U.S. Marshal Service. Will had no intention of working within the law to find the man he wanted. He'd do it his way, no matter the consequences.

Five years ago he never would've considered going outside of the law. Five years ago he would've been helping his brothers prepare for winter, and Emily would've been getting ready to deliver their baby. Aunt Alicia, Niall's wife, Kate, and Jamie's wife, Torie, would've been driving all the men crazy with their plans for the new arrival. Niall and Kate had a boy, Adam. Jamie and Torie also had a boy, Isaac. Everyone had wondered if he and Emily would bring the first girl into the family since the birth of Niall's daughter, Beth, who was now fourteen. He hadn't cared. He'd only wanted the one thing that God hadn't provided, a healthy child and wife.

But he had relented when June McAllister pestered him to get a message off to his Aunt Alicia. The telegraph Sam sent with the job offer for Cord had included a warning that Alicia MacLaren had reached her limit. She hadn't heard from her nephew in months. It'd be best for everyone if he could get Will to contact his family.

A hearty crack of lightening brought Will out of his reminiscing. His stallion, Justice, pranced sideways at the sudden sound. Will could see lights ahead and urged his horse forward but it took another hour before he reached the outskirts of Cold Creek. He needed to find a livery, food, and the sheriff, in that order. Then he could locate a bed and get out of his soaked clothes. The livery and food were easy. The sheriff wasn't in his office and not at his home the town provided behind the jail. He'd have to wait for morning. Sleep sounded real good.

******

"Sheriff?"

The bulky man sitting behind the desk scouring wanted-posters looked up. "Yea. What can I do for you?" A slight southern accent tinged his deep voice.

"Wondered if you might know where I could find Chet Hollis. I believe he lives in this area. I've come up from New Mexico looking for him." Will's voice was friendly but hard, the ever-present rasp growing worse in cold weather. Just thinking of Hollis made the anger that was his constant companion rise to the surface.

The sheriff's head shot up at the mention of the name, but he controlled his alarm. "That so. And what do you want with him?"

Will didn't respond. Instead, he opened the old wanted poster and placed it on the sheriff's desk. He waited while the older man reviewed the document, rubbed his hand across his unshaven face, then looked up.

"This poster says Chad Hawley. Don't think you got the right man, uh..."

"MacLaren. Will MacLaren."

Again, the sheriff worked to control his shock as his mind registered the name. "Well, MacLaren, don't think this Hawley is Chet Hollis. Chet's been around here, oh, three or four years. He's clean-shaven with real short hair. Stockier than the man in this poster." The sheriff shook his head and handed the poster back to Will. "Sorry, MacLaren. Can't help you."

"Well, I'll be checking him out anyway, Sheriff. Thanks for your time." Will opened the door to leave.

"MacLaren?"

"Yea?"

"You wouldn't be related to a Marshal Jamie MacLaren, would you?"

"He's my brother." Will closed the door behind him.

Chapter Four

"Over there, Amanda." Joey pointed toward the errant cow from atop the big roan he loved to ride. Jester had been given to him on his fifth birthday. He couldn't quite fit the horse, even at ten, but he sure could handle him. Joey circled the stranded heifer while pulling out his rope. The poor thing had become entangled in the thick brush on the banks of the Gundy, and couldn't get her footing to climb out. If she'd been any younger he and Amanda could've just lifted her up the bank, but that wasn't going to happen now.

"Okay, Joey, throw me the rope." Amanda dismounted to climb down the embankment. Slipping the rope around the heifer's neck, she moved behind the animal to help push. "Joey, pull real slow and steady. I'll push and we'll see if we can get her started."

A minute later Amanda was waist deep in river water with mud in her boots and a nervous heifer struggling to get traction on the gooey bank.

"Need some help, ma'am?"

Amanda looked up to see a man on a beautiful black horse dismounting while Joey kept hold of the rope.

"Wouldn't want you to drown saving a cow, right?" He began working his way down the bank to the back of the animal. Within seconds he had her moving up the bank and on to dry ground.

Standing, he brushed his dirty hands on his pants and started back up the slope.

"Aren't you going to help Amanda up, mister?" Joey took the rope off the heifer and stared up at the imposing figure.

"Nope. Doesn't look to me like she needs any help." He glanced behind him as he climbed back on his horse.

Before he could turn the stallion to leave, Amanda walked toward him, pushed her hair out of her face, looked up, and smiled. It was a broad and utterly radiant smile that drew his gaze up to the most magnificent, bright-blue eyes he'd ever seen, like the blue in the English china Aunt Alicia had at home.

"I just want to thank you, Mister..." Amanda held out her hand.

He took it reluctantly. "Will, ma'am. Will MacLaren. Glad I could help." Her hand felt good in his. Too good.

"I'm Amanda Taylor and this is my brother, Joey." She hesitated only a moment when he withdrew his hand abruptly. "Well, um, my brother and I couldn't seem to get it accomplished. It would've taken us forever," she stammered, not knowing what to say next.

"Like I said, glad I could help." He nodded to both, then turned Justice toward the ranch across the valley. Amanda just stared at his retreating figure.

"Who was that, Amanda?"

"Just some man named Will MacLaren. Never saw him before." Amanda let out a breath she didn't know she'd been holding. "Well, let's get ourselves home and cleaned up. Maria will have supper waiting for us, and you know how she is when we're late."

******

"I told you, Chet, the man is asking questions, and I don't believe anything I said changed his mind about you being the man on the poster. Heard he was heading out to the Taylor place—don't know why, but they're looking for men. Maybe you ought to go out there, talk with him. Convince him you're not the man he's after and put his suspicions to rest. Encourage him to move along." Sweat beaded on the sheriff's forehead and his hands shook. He placed the warm beer he'd been holding back on the table. He didn't know why he drank the stuff, except it wasn't coffee, his other drink of choice. "We can't afford to have him poking around, asking questions about you."

"Now, Ellis, you worry too much. It's been five years and we've been here three of them. No one's going to believe I'm the person on the poster. Hell, the man's looking for someone who killed a woman—a pregnant woman at that—and left the husband for dead. You think the good people of Cold Creek would ever believe I'd do something like that?" Chet took a sip of his whiskey and peered over the rim of the glass to gauge Dutton's reaction. He couldn't let the man panic and ruin everything. "He'll never be able to prove I'm the same person. Take my word for it." Chet had no plans to confront MacLaren. No, he'd wait until he could catch the bounty hunter unawares, then kill

38

him and dispose of the body. Might even get rid of Dutton at the same time.

The sheriff thought he saw something in the other man's eyes but couldn't be sure. He'd need to keep an eye on Chet, just in case. They shared many secrets, and he sure as hell wasn't going to go take the blame for the man's past crimes. What they'd been doing was bad enough, but murder? "That's not all. Do you have any idea who his brother is?" When Chet didn't respond, Dutton continued. "Jamie MacLaren. He was a U.S. Marshal, one of the best. Fast with a gun and never gave up when he was after someone. He and his brother are a lot alike, it appears. They're a bad pair, Chet. This bounty hunter is someone you need to deal with, and soon. You got that?"

Chet ignored the warning. "Like I said, it's been too long for him to prove a thing. As far as anyone knows, I'm just a hired hand out at Bierdan's ranch, that's all." Chet downed the last of his whiskey and stood. "Don't let his presence spook you. We're both just what we appear to be, nothing more."

Hollis mounted his horse for the ride back to the Bierdan ranch and thought about the conversation with Dutton. Five years of being careful, working at menial jobs, laying low, and now this. Of course, he'd done a few other things during that time—including the side job he and Dutton had been doing the past year—but no more killing. His life had changed after that day in Fire Mountain. But he'd always known he could become that man again if pushed, and MacLaren might just be the man who could do the pushing.

Chet had plans that included Miss Taylor and staying in Cold Creek. No one was going to drive him away from what he wanted, and he wanted that woman. He sure as hell wouldn't let some bounty hunter—the husband of the woman he had murdered—haul him in now and ruin all he'd worked for. He'd kill again before he'd let that happen.

******

"And where have you two been?" Maria, their long-time housekeeper and cook, asked as soon as Amanda and Joey walked in the back door.

"Had trouble with a cow, Maria." Joey glanced at his sister and laughed, then shot up the stairs to change clothes.

"She was stuck in the river bank and couldn't get out. Pushed me into the river, too, but we were fortunate. A rider happened by and helped us out." Amanda smiled at the memory of the good-looking man on his magnificent black horse. She couldn't put her finger on what it was about the stranger that had her on edge. She only knew that she'd never felt like this around anyone else—a combination of excitement and dread, all at once. "So, what's for supper?" Amanda needed to change, get some food, and then work on the books before heading to bed. All that would help keep her thoughts off Will MacLaren.

The back door banged open. "Hey, Maria. What's for supper?" Jake called as he removed his dirty boots and set them beside the door.

"Stew and biscuits with berry pie for dessert, just like I said this afternoon," Maria grumbled, and rolled her eyes at his dirty clothes. They had known each other for years and for all that time she and Jake had kept up this constant stream of crotchety banter. He smiled at the slight aggravation in her voice. They both knew he came to supper with dirty clothes just to get a rise out of her. He'd never do that if Amanda's mother, Eleanor, were here to enforce her form of English etiquette.

"All right, you two, let's start supper. I'm starving." Amanda descended the stairs to take her place at the table.

Ranch life produced an appetite that Amanda had never experienced back East. At school, young ladies were expected to take small portions and eat even smaller amounts than what they took. For some incongruous reason, leaving food on your plate was expected in that world. That had never been the situation on the ranch. You ate the animals you raised and the plants you grew, and did not let food go to waste. Looking back, she didn't know how she'd made it through without losing more weight. Her father had been shocked to see her very slim figure when she had first returned home. Within a couple of months, she had put back on all the weight she'd lost while at school.

"Hired that new hand we've been needing. Think he's going to work out great. Used to work for a large spread in Arizona. From what I can tell, man knows his stuff," Jake said between bites.

"That's great. How'd you meet him?" One more thing Amanda didn't have to worry about. Many of the hands moved south over the winter, choosing warmer locations over the cold, snow-packed winters.

"He rode up today. Had several letters of reference from ranchers, as well as one from the sheriff in Splitshot, New Mexico, and another from the sheriff in Fire Mountain, Arizona. Rode in on one of the most impressive black stallions I've ever seen. Would you pass the stew, please, Maria?" Jake finished without seeing how his words had affected Amanda.

"A big black stallion with a white blaze?" Joey asked, also unaware of how Jake's words had impacted his sister.

"Yea. How'd you know?" Jake passed the rest of the stew over to Joey for him to finish.

"He's the stranger who helped us with the heifer this afternoon." Joey finished off the stew while grabbing another biscuit.

"What heifer?" Jake looked at Amanda and set down his fork while Amanda explained the happenings by the river.

"He introduced himself as Will MacLaren." Amanda folded her napkin before standing to walk towards the kitchen. "Who wants pie?" She asked over her shoulder as she disappeared into the next room.

Amanda reached up to grab plates from the cupboard. *Will MacLaren*, she thought. Of all the men Jake could have hired, it had to be the one person who unsettled her more than anyone she'd ever known, and she'd only just met the man. Well, she had a ranch to run, a brother to help raise, and so many other duties around the Big G to take care of while her parents were away that she would just make it a point to stay as far away from MacLaren as she could.

Chapter Five

"Good morning, Mr. MacLaren. Jake told me he had hired you to work the Big G." Amanda smiled as she turned to stare up, yet again, at the broad-shouldered, imposing figure of Will MacLaren as he entered the barn. "Where does he have you working today?"

"The usual." He took off his hat and ran the other hand through his auburn colored hair. He cast a disinterested gaze around the barn as if comparing it to something else. "Riding fences, looking for strays———or anything unusual."

"I see. Is that what you did at the other ranches?" So many things about this stranger intrigued Amanda, including the rough, raspy tone of his voice. *Was he born that way, or was he injured?* What was it about this man that aroused her curiosity?

"Yes, among other things." He stared into her eyes for the first time that morning, then glanced away. "I better get going, Miss Taylor." Will turned his back on her and strode to Justice's stall.

Amanda stared at the retreating figure. She wasn't used to people snubbing her, especially not ranch hands, or ignoring a question as simple as where he had gotten his experience. But he'd looked uncomfortable the minute she'd asked about other ranches and had taken the first opportunity to shut down their conversation. *Why?* Amanda thought as she mounted Angel to ride south and survey the river area for the second day in a row.

"Amanda, wait up." Jake walked out of the bunkhouse toward her. "I'd like you to ride with MacLaren today. Give him a tour of the ranch, boundaries, and such. Planned to take him myself, but we're having a problem with a couple of the new colts and I'm needed here."

"I don't believe Mr. MacLaren needs any help from me or anyone." Amanda still stung from the rebuff by the new hand. "He's a loner, Jake. I'm sure he's good, just like you said, but a loner all the same. Send one of the boys with him if you think he needs a nursemaid." She cast a look over her shoulder at the barn just in time to see Will leading Justice outside.

"Now, Amanda." Jake could only smile at the defiance in Amanda's voice. He didn't know a more affable woman, and polite to a fault, but keep out of her way if she felt slighted. "He couldn't have gotten you so riled this quick, could he? Or is something else tainting your day? And so early, too." He grinned at the disgust on her face.

"No one's riled me. I just have my own plans, that's all, and they do not include the new hand. Find someone else. Please."

"All right, but I'm sending Joey your way as soon as he finishes his studies," Jake yelled after her. "You hear me, girl?"

All Jake got was a wave of her hand as she continued south and away from the stranger who both annoyed and fascinated her.

******

45

The Bierdan ranch lay over the ridge in front of him and abutted the Taylor spread on the west for several miles. Although not as large as the Big G, the locals told him the only place more successful than the Bierdan ranch was Grant Taylor's spread. Will had learned that Chet Hollis had been working for Gordon Bierdan for at least two years. Best he could figure, others respected Chet as a ranch hand, even if he was a hothead and braggart. No one seemed to particularly like him. Will had been told Chet hung out with a man named Wiley, who also worked at the Bierdan place. Wiley seemed to be the one to help Chet out of sticky situations and keep relations with other ranchers on good terms. Perhaps Will could get him to open up about Hollis.

He'd ignored Jake's request that he ride with one of the boys to get to know the land. Will had his own agenda for the day, and it didn't include tagging along with another ranch hand.

Will planned to ride the fence line from one end of the common boundary to the other, keeping an eye on the happenings below, and figure out the best way to isolate Hawley, or Hollis, as he now called himself. There was no real hurry. Even if Hawley got wind of MacLaren being in the area, where would he go? Will would be on his tail without a backward glance, and this time he'd get the bastard who killed Emily.

She had been the sweetest person he'd ever known. Funny and bright, she always knew just what to do when he was angry, or confused, as he'd often been between the time he had met her at thirteen and their marriage several years later. Everyone had loved her, and why wouldn't they? She was the most giving person he'd ever known, with a huge heart and boundless energy. And for a time, she had been his, and his future had seemed limitless. Now? Well, there wasn't any future, and wouldn't be until Emily's killer was brought to justice. *Soon, Emily,* he thought. *It will be real soon now.*

Chapter Six

Denver, Colorado

"Hey, Mr. MacLaren!" Drew heard the shout from down the street and turned to see his secretary hurrying after him. Drew MacLaren had graduated from Columbia School of Law. He had taken a position at a large, prestigious firm in New York City for a few years, reviewing and preparing business contracts, but then decided his heart was still rooted in the land, in ranching. He was fortunate. One of his largest clients in New York owned holdings in silver mines and ranches in Colorado. Louis Dunnigan needed someone to handle all of his legal issues out of the state capitol of Denver. He wanted a man who understood the differences between East Coast society and the more primitive culture of the West, as both skills would be required for success. And, Dunnigan needed someone who'd be willing to move west for the opportunity. Drew jumped at the chance. Over a year into the move, he was still pleased with his decision.

"Good morning, Terrance. What can I do for you?" Drew stopped to wait for the older man to catch up.

"Message from Splitshot, New Mexico. Labeled urgent, so I thought it best to deliver it post-haste, sir." Terrance handed Drew the message and waited for a response.

Splitshot? Now who did he know in that part of New Mexico? Then it clicked. Cord McAllister. Drew opened the message and read through it a couple of times before looking down at the shorter man who was standing, waiting.

"Would you like me to send a response for you, sir?" He spoke in a crisp, no nonsense voice. He had excellent credentials, impeccable taste in clothes, and a long history with Dunnigan Enterprises, but he always seemed to be just a little too polished for Denver, the West in general, and especially for Drew.

"No thank you, Terrance. I'll handle this one myself." He was already contemplating the implied consequences of the message from his old friend.

"As you wish, Mr. MacLaren," Terrance said, but saw that his boss had already turned to walk down the street.

******

Chet Hollis decided to bide his time, learn more about Will MacLaren, and, most important, learn how to shield himself from whatever the bounty hunter had in mind. Hollis had known MacLaren was the husband of the woman he'd murdered. He'd learned it soon afterwards, but, at the time, his only thoughts were to ride out of the territory, lose himself, and not look back. Had he known how persistent the man would be at pursuing him, even after everyone else had accepted the false report of his death, he'd have left another body behind in Fire Mountain, not just an injured man.

Things had gone bad that day for Chad Hawley, now known as Chet Hollis. His Pa, brothers, and several members of their gang had busted Hawley out of a small jail, about a half-day's ride from Fire Mountain. They'd stopped at a saloon in the booming ranching area, eaten, gotten liquored up, and then ridden north out of town when word started to spread that an outlaw had broken out of jail in Watsonville, wounding the deputy.

They were all feeling good—too good, given their dire circumstances—but liquor had a way of turning their heads, making them crazy. The brothers continued to share a bottle of whiskey as they rode. Their Pa wasn't happy with their defiance of his order to throw it away. He watched as their behavior continued to deteriorate. Several miles outside of Fire Mountain, their Pa spotted a wagon crossing not far in front of them. He held up his hand for them to hold up, wait until it passed, but Chad saw that one of the passengers was a woman, and he hadn't had a woman in a long time.

The brothers ignored their Pa and raced each other towards the unsuspecting couple. Before long the man was shot and pulled out of the wagon, and Chad had the woman in the brush off the road, pulling up her dress while she screamed and threw punches at his face, hands, neck, anywhere she could get purchase. She screamed that she was pregnant, but he ignored her, continuing his savage attack.

Her rebelliousness angered him even as it fired up his need for her to a feverish pitch. He took what he wanted, his hands wrapped around her throat to stop her screams. Chad's hands stilled when her screams ceased, and it was then he saw her vacant eyes. Panic overtook him. He pushed away, mounted his horse, and the group of riders raced from the carnage.

His Pa had decided to split the group up, with Chad going one direction and the rest of them heading another. He'd thrown a couple of bags of coin on the floor and ridden out the following morning, leaving Chad to his own fate. Over the following months Chad heard that his Pa had been gunned down in Utah, his brothers tried and hung in Arizona, and the other members of the gang arrested or killed. He was the only one left. MacLaren was the man who'd tracked them all down.

He devised the plan to get himself "killed" in Santa Fe with the cooperation of a deputy willing to help him out for a financial contribution. Everyone had accepted Chad Hawley's death as real. Afterwards, Chet Hollis rode out of Santa Fe and never looked back.

The deputy who'd assisted him in Santa Fe quit his job shortly after Hawley's reported death. They met up in a small New Mexico town, then headed north, through parts of Utah and Colorado, robbing when needed, until they found Cold Creek. The town needed a sheriff, and Ellis Dutton jumped at the opportunity to hide out in the mountain location. A local rancher needed a wrangler and Chet Hollis and settled into a normal life as a ranch hand for Gordon Bierdan. After almost three years, he'd thought he was finally safe, but MacLaren had found him. The man just didn't give up. He didn't know how to walk away. Well, Hollis wasn't going to run again. He'd find MacLaren's weakness and get rid of him for good.

******

Will spent the entire day canvassing the Bierdan ranch without spotting Hollis or Wiley. Fact was, most of the men were absent, out riding fences or looking for strays. His years of ranch experience enabled Will to repair fence lines while rounding up half a dozen strays and still watching over the neighboring ranch. He hadn't held a ranching job in over two years, and truth be told, it felt good. It all came so naturally. It was something he'd been born to do, as Niall and Jamie often reminded him.

Niall was good at the long-term strategy and politics of growing a large ranching empire. Jamie had connections throughout the West. After years of being a U.S. Marshal, he was highly respected and no one disputed his expertise with a gun. Drew was the scholar of the bunch, heading off to college, then law school, before settling in Denver.

Will had been the true rancher of the group. After Emily, his love had always been the land, the cattle, and horses. At least they had been five years ago. His brothers and aunt had begged him to give up his quest and come home. He knew they needed him, but it just wasn't time. Maybe it never would be.

"We were beginning to give up on you. Thought the work might be too hard and you took off," Jake joked when Will rode up with his small herd of stray cattle. "Looks like you had some success. Put those in here for tonight." He pointed toward the open gate and small, fenced pasture. "We'll join them up with the main herd north of here tomorrow."

Will did as Jake ordered, but didn't speak. Just moved the cattle through the gate, turned towards the barn, and disappeared inside.

After securing the pen, Jake followed Will. "Amanda saved your dinner, if you want to head into the house." After no response from Will, Jake continued. "Don't even think about refusing, as she don't take kindly to making supper and people not showing up. That one hates to waste anything, most of all food."

Will looked at the foreman, mumbled his thanks, and headed toward the house. The last person Will wanted to see was Amanda. He didn't know what it was about her, but she conjured up feelings that had no place in his life, and, from what he could tell, he elicited the same feelings in her. But even if they acted on them, there was no future in a relationship with anyone, least of all the daughter of a prominent Colorado rancher. If he ever did end his life as a bounty hunter, he'd return home, to Fire Mountain and his family.

"Mr. MacLaren. Glad you could make it." Irritation tinged her voice as Amanda motioned for him to have a seat at the small table in the kitchen and placed a large plate, filled to over-flowing, in front of him. He'd thought he wasn't hungry, but smelling the food and looking at his plate made his stomach growl. Jerky and hardtack only went so far when you worked as hard as he had today.

"Thank you, ma'am," Will murmured and attacked the food before him.

Amanda let him eat in silence while she finished cleaning up the pots and stacking them under the counter. Maria had been given the day off, leaving the house responsibilities to Amanda. It had been a long day. When she glanced at the man at the table, she realized for the first time that he looked as tired as she felt, and knew he must be exhausted. She turned her back to him, more to stop staring than to finish the few remaining dishes. After a while, Amanda heard the sound of silverware scraping an empty plate.

"Thanks again, ma'am." He walked to the sink to clean his plate.

"I'll take that, Mr. MacLaren. You're free to head out." Amanda took the plate from his hand. Her fingers brushed his, and she stilled at the surge of electricity that shot up her arm at the brief touch. She looked up to stare into clear, hazel eyes. He stood well over six-feet-tall and was the most ruggedly handsome man she'd ever seen.

Will couldn't take his eyes off of her. Her deep blue eyes sparkled with hints of green. They were welcoming eyes that drew him to her. Her raven black hair had been pulled back into a loose bun at the nape of her neck. He wanted to reach out and pull the pins from it to see how it would look falling over her shoulders. His exhaustion couldn't stop him from wondering what it would be like to find someone again, maybe someone like Amanda, and settle down. His daydreams froze on that last thought and he broke eye contact.

"Thanks again, Miss Taylor. I appreciate you holding some food for me." He strolled to the back door.

"Mr. MacLaren?" Amanda called after him.

Will turned, not sure what to expect.

"Don't count on it happening again. Everyone eats on time here, so I expect you'll be at the table with everyone else tomorrow. Understand?"

"Yes, ma'am." Will tipped his hat and walked through the door into the cool night air. As he started toward the bunkhouse a slight smile curved his usually grim mouth. He hadn't realized until now what a foreign feeling a smile had become. Well, he wouldn't become used to it, he told himself, but Amanda Taylor sure did have a way about her.

Chapter Seven

Fire Mountain, Arizona

"What's the message say, Jamie?" Aunt Alicia asked when Jamie just stared at the paper he held. Jamie, Torie, their young son, Isaac, and Aunt Alicia had come into Fire Mountain for supplies. Torie's parents owned the general store, as well as the largest hotel in town, and the bulk of their supplies were always ready to pick up each Saturday. Today, however, his in-laws and aunt were going to visit and watch Isaac while he took his wife to lunch at Mattie's. Even though the family would celebrate Torie's birthday at home tonight, he wanted to do something special. Tom, from the telegraph office, had intercepted him just as he and Torie were leaving the store.

"It's from Cord McAllister, in New Mexico. Will thinks he's found the last man, Chad Hawley, and is tracking him to Cold Creek, Colorado." Jamie looked up to see the concern on his aunt's face. They all knew if Will found Hawley, he was just as apt to kill him outright as to take him in for trial.

"My God." Alicia's right hand came up to cover her mouth. The rest of the family had thought Hawley dead, killed years ago in Santa Fe, but Will had never believed it and had refused to give up the search after learning that no one in Santa Fe, except one deputy, had seen the body. The deputy quit his job days after declaring Hawley dead, left Santa Fe, and no one had heard from him again. Jamie had also thought it didn't sound right, but no one had any proof otherwise. Maybe Will had been correct all along when he'd told them he thought it had been a setup. He always did have incredible instincts.

"Are you planning to go to Cold Creek, Jamie?" Torie asked. She was six months pregnant with their second child and the last thing Jamie wanted to do was leave her.

"I don't know. I need to speak with Niall before I make a decision. Cord indicated he already sent word to Drew, so we'll contact him, also–––get his thoughts." Jamie sighed. He'd never lost hope Will would return home to the ranch. Now dread consumed him, knowing what the message might mean.

"We'll ride back to the ranch, then." Torie turned to find Isaac and say good-bye to her folks.

"But lunch, your birthday..." Jamie said.

Torie looked back at her husband, concern for her brother-in-law etched on her face. "This is much more important. I'll have my birthday dinner tonight, while we all talk about how to find Will and bring him home."

******

"Will, I'd like you to go with Amanda and Joey into town. Help them with supplies and pick up any messages. Mr. Taylor tries to keep us posted on his travels, but we haven't heard anything in several weeks." Jake limped towards Will and the other men who were taking their Saturday morning coffee outside the bunkhouse.

"Get one of the others to go, Jake. I've got plans." Will didn't even look up from his coffee, just kept blowing on the hot brew to cool it down.

"I asked you, MacLaren, and you're the one who'll go." Jake had no problem with the men having plans on their own days, but Saturday was considered a work day, and the others already had their work laid out. "Besides, Sheriff Dutton sent a man out yesterday, asking to speak with you. You had already ridden out, so I told him you'd see the sheriff today. Just makes sense you take Amanda and Joey with you."

"What the hell happened to you, Boss?" Tinder, one of the youngest hands, hadn't noticed Jake's injured leg until now.

"Fell off his horse. Didn't you know that, Tin?" Frank Alts had been at the ranch just a couple of months and had become friends with Tinder and his buddy, Johnny Mullins. Tinder and Johnny had signed on together at the Big G a few years before. They'd taken a liking to Alts and now the three rode together most days.

"Nothing any of you need to concern yourself with. Isn't it about time you all finished your coffee and got going?" Jake looked at his pocket watch. "It's almost six and you're all sitting here like society ladies. Now, get moving." Jake turned toward the barn, but looking over his shoulder he spotted Will still sitting on the step. "You, too, MacLaren. Wagon doesn't hitch itself."

Hell, Will thought as he poured his half finished coffee on the ground and followed the

58

foreman to the barn. He had plans and they didn't include watching over the young mistress and her brother. Would've been better to send Tinder or Alts with them. Much to Will's disgust, Tinder had seldom taken his eyes off Miss Taylor since Will had arrived. It irritated him when the other men watched Amanda with too much interest, but damned if he understood why. He needed distance from her, not the forced closeness of a day fetching supplies in town.

Fifteen minutes later the wagon was out front of the house. Will had Justice saddled, and glanced up to see Jake and several other men leaving for the south pasture. Jake had assumed Will would ride with Amanda and Joey in the wagon, but Will had other ideas. It would just be too tight for three people, and much too close for him and Miss Taylor.

"Mr. MacLaren." Amanda acknowledged him while descending the steps to board the wagon. Joey came flying out a minute later, jumped into the wagon, and grabbed the reins.

"Good morning, Miss Taylor, Joey," Will said. "You two ready?"

"Yep," Joey replied then tapped the horses with the reins to start the trip.

Three hours later all the supplies were loaded. While Amanda and Joey left for lunch, Will walked to the telegraph office for any messages. Sure enough, Mr. Taylor had sent one to Jake, and another to Joey and Amanda. The third message was for one of the hands. He'd just turned to leave when the clerk called to him.

"Hey. You MacLaren?"

"That's me."

"Got one more message here for you."

Will walked back to the desk and grabbed the message from the man's outstretched hand. It was from Drew. How the hell did Drew know he was in Cold Creek? Will read the message twice, swore softly under his breath, then grabbed paper and pen to quickly craft a reply. After handing it to the operator and paying the fee, he headed toward the restaurant and his own lunch, alone.

"MacLaren."

Will saw the portly man amble across the main street towards him. He'd completely forgotten the summons to stop by the jail.

"Sheriff. What can I do for you?"

"Got a couple more questions for you, if you have the time, of course." Both men knew this wasn't a request. The sheriff looked like a man ready to explode and most likely at Will.

"Sure. Where do you want to talk?"

"My office would be best, then you can go about your day."

Once inside the office, the sheriff motioned for Will to take a seat before launching into his soft spoken but hard edged tirade. "Is there a reason you didn't tell me that Chad Hawley died more than three years ago in Santa Fe?"

Will thought about the disappearance of the deputy right after Hawley had been reported dead. Nothing illegal about the deputy coming up missing, but the coincidence was curious. "Chad Hawley wasn't killed in Santa Fe. In fact, a few days after the body was found, they realized a drifter was also missing, but they'd already had the burial. Never could determine for sure that it was Hawley in the grave. Even the sheriff admitted all the circumstances seemed strange, but because it was his deputy who'd reported seeing the killing, and identified the body, he was forced to show the death as Hawley's."

Dutton listened to Will's story. He knew for a fact that the bounty hunter had it right. Hawley had murdered the drifter and Dutton had identified the body as Hawley's. The sheriff knew he was taking a chance talking with MacLaren, but he needed to understand how much the man knew. He knew a lot.

"Sounds like a bunch of guessing to me." Dutton wanted to find a way to throw the man off, get him to move on before Hawley did something stupid. If it came down to it, Dutton would quit his job and leave his partner to his own fate. The sheriff knew he could get a job in another small town where he'd never be associated with the killer. He'd lose what they'd been working for, but at least he'd keep his life.

"Believe what you will. Hawley is Chet Hollis, and I'll prove it before I leave Cold Creek. And when I leave, I'll either take Hollis with me, or leave him here for you to bury." MacLaren's voice was hard, unwavering. He knew his search would end in this small Colorado town.

******

Amanda couldn't sleep. She tossed around, pushed off the covers, tugged them back up, stared at the ceiling a while, and finally grabbed the book next to her bed. The cause was obvious. She couldn't get her mind off their new ranch hand. Amanda had sat in the wagon all the way to town and back, watching him and the image he made riding his beautiful horse. Muscular legs and a soft hand controlled the animal with little effort. She'd found herself wondering what MacLaren would look like without a shirt, sweat on his chest and back from working. He was broad shouldered, and by all appearances, someone you wouldn't want to rile. Amanda concluded that he'd be magnificent. She knew her thoughts were headed in a dangerous direction but her mind wouldn't shut down.

Throwing back the covers, Amanda got out of bed and snatched her wrapper from the wardrobe before heading down the stairs to the kitchen. Warm milk always made her sleepy and she needed whatever help she could get to stop thinking about the much-too-handsome wrangler.

She reached the kitchen just as an odd sound came from outside. Amanda continued to pour milk into a pan until she heard the sound again. What was that noise? It came from behind the house, just around the corner from where she stood looking out the kitchen window. The noise continued until she couldn't ignore it any longer. She shoved her feet into boots, grabbed the rifle, and stepped outside, into a clear, chilled night. Fall was one of the best times of year, just before snow blanketed the area for several months. It wouldn't be long now before chores and travel would be much more complicated.

Amanda followed the sound until she stood just at the corner of the house and peered around. What she saw stopped her cold. MacLaren stood not ten feet away, without a shirt, chopping and piling wood at what seemed a frantic pace. Each time he'd raise the ax the muscles of his back and arms would tighten, creating one of the most exciting visions she'd ever seen. She rested the rifle against the side of the house and watched for several moments, mesmerized by the sight before her. He was just as she'd imagined. Her gaze intensified with each movement until she couldn't break the spell and could barely breathe.

He felt rather than saw her behind him and waited for Amanda to announce her presence, but she said nothing.

"You just going to stand back there and stare at my half naked body, Miss Taylor?"

Amanda jumped at his sudden words.

Will set down the ax, picked up his shirt, and turned to face her. He wasn't prepared for the image before him. She wore a simple wrapper over her nightgown, and the full moon cast shadows through both layers of thin fabric. Her silky black hair was fashioned in one long braid that had fallen over her left shoulder, covering one breast. His mouth went dry and he worked to control his breathing. She was an extraordinary vision.

He took a deep breath and forced his gaze to her eyes. "What can I do for you, Miss Taylor? Did you need something from me?"

"I...well..." She couldn't force the words out—they'd become locked in her throat.

"Yes?" Will chuckled at her obvious discomfort.

She recovered when she realized he found the situation humorous. "I heard noise and came to check it out. Why are you out here, chopping wood so late? It's after midnight, Mr. MacLaren."

"Couldn't sleep. I often can't, and need to do something physical to calm my mind. Any problem with that?" He continued to let his eyes roam over her beautiful form as the wind whipped the fabric around her legs and the folds clung to her body. She'd become a stunning sculpture. He tried to drag his eyes away, but found he could not.

Although he'd slipped into his shirt, he had yet to close the buttons. She couldn't keep her eyes off his broad chest, peppered with reddish brown hair and tanned from working in the sun. Breathing became more labored as each second passed and she had difficulty swallowing.

Will watched her eyes as they traveled from his chest up to his neck, then to his face. What he saw in those eyes pulled him back to the present. "Miss Taylor, did you hear me?"

"Um, yes, I mean no. What did you say?" She felt foolish and needed to get back into the house before she acted on her irrational and reckless impulse to walk up and touch him, feel his skin beneath her hands.

"I think you'd best get back in the house where it's warm, Miss Taylor. I'm finished here. The noise won't disturb you any longer."

Amanda managed to pull her eyes from him long enough to control her raging thoughts and focus on his words. "Yes, it is a little chilly." She rubbed her hands up and down her arms. "Well, good night, Mr. MacLaren." Amanda reached for the rifle and, cradling it gently, walked back into the house.

"Good night, Miss Taylor."

But each lay in their bed without sleep until the early morning hours, trying to calm the unanticipated desire that had sprung up between them––a desire that neither had the slightest notion how to stop.

******

"Amanda, I want you to ride out with MacLaren this morning and show him the spots where we think the cattle have gone missing. You know where I mean." Even though her parents owned the ranch, Jake still ran the operations while they were gone, and assigned the jobs each day.

"All right, but you know he won't be happy about it." It had become clear to everyone that the ranch-hand was a loner who didn't want or appreciate others tagging along when he worked.

"Yeah, well, he's the hired hand and I'm the foreman, so he'll have to get used to taking the orders I hand out. Besides, I already told him and he's waiting for you at the barn." Jake turned back to the sink to toss out the last drops of coffee.

"And, Joey?" After last night, Amanda didn't want to work alone with MacLaren all day. She needed her brother to tag along, provide a barrier and a distraction.

"I've already got him working with Tinder, Johnny, and Frank, so it'll have to be just the two of you." Jake looked at her a moment, wondering at the anxious tone in her voice. "You okay this morning, Amanda? You seem a little unsettled."

Yes, she was unsettled, but she didn't want Jake to know it or learn why. "No, I'm fine, just didn't sleep too well." She pulled on her boots and started for the door. "See you in a few hours."

******

"So he knows the truth, does he?" Hollis wasn't surprised, but had hoped he'd be able to find a way to convince the bounty hunter he wasn't the man he sought.

"That he does and he means to stay until he proves you're Hawley. Doesn't matter to him if you go back alive or in a box, but I'm guessing the box would be his first choice." Dutton was scared and didn't mind if Hollis knew it. MacLaren was a danger to both of them and the sheriff had no intention of staying around to get caught in the crossfire. "We've got to move the cattle we have, sell them, and get out of here. Leave before he gets the proof he needs. We can start over somewhere else, further north, some place he won't think to look."

Hollis turned on his partner and shoved him against the wall. "Now you hear me and hear me good. We aren't leaving until we've got the number of head needed to make good money. He won't drive me out and if I stay, you stay." He let go of Dutton and stepped back a few feet. "As for the

66

cattle, there's no way to rid ourselves of them without raising suspicions. The herd is a good size and holed up in a big valley with only one way in and out. No one will find them. Wiley's with us and so is our man at the Taylor ranch. Between the four of us and the other men we'll keep the cattle fed and safe. Anyway, we can't move them until the boss has everything ready."

"Damn it, Chet, who is this boss you keep talking about who's pulling the strings? I want to meet him. We've never needed anyone before and I still don't know why you brought someone else into it. Who is he?" Ellis Dutton had been blind-sided several weeks before when Hollis had told him he'd hooked up with someone with money, power, and connections in Denver. But the man wanted to run the operation, call the shots, and use Chet and Ellis as the front men. The sheriff knew the man must have something on Chet or he never would've let the man take over. Ellis didn't like any of it. "Take me to see him, talk some sense into him. Don't you see, it's just not worth the risk? MacLaren's gotten every one of those involved in his wife's death. He won't back down until he gets the last one—you. We aren't safe here."

"You may be right, but we aren't changing anything yet." Hollis refused to back-off. They were too close to getting what they wanted. Besides, the man who'd forced himself into their plans would never agree to closing up until all the cattle he wanted were safely tucked away. Hollis knew he could die at the hands of the bounty hunter, but he'd be just as dead if he challenged the other man. "Besides, I've got plans and they include staying in Cold Creek, and building on the land we bought up river. I'm going to have a regular life, be respected, even if I have to get rid of that bounty hunter to do it."

Dutton paced to the window and watched the clouds obscure the sun, darkening the sky as a slight mist began. "You'll never get her, you know. She'll never marry someone like you even if her Pa would allow it, and we both know he won't."

"Yeah, well, he's not here to protect her. She has the one old foreman and a few decent hands, but none I can't take down if needed."

"And MacLaren? He's part of the Big G now."

"Understand this, Dutton. I'll do whatever it takes to have her, and that means getting rid of anyone who gets in my way, including the bounty hunter."

Chapter Eight

"Where to now, Miss Taylor?" Will's voice was hard, devoid of any inflection. He was more than ready for the morning to be over so they could return to the ranch. He needed to get away from Amanda—far away. Neither had mentioned the night before, but it hung between them like a dense fog.

They'd dismounted and were resting under some large pines. Riding for three hours straight without a break wasn't uncommon, but today it was just too long. Amanda pulled out a sack from her saddlebags and shared the cold chicken and biscuits with Will. He needed this distraction.

"As far as I know, there are only two more places where we seem to lose cattle, then we can head back. I don't want to be out here with you any more than you want to be with me. The sooner we're done, the better I'll feel." She was tired from lack of sleep and the constant tension. She'd never felt this way before around a man, not even the man she'd planned to marry.

"Miss Taylor, about last night..."

"I don't want to speak of it, Mr. MacLaren. Let's just forget about it, all right?" Talking would only conjure up images of the man beside her. Images she'd like to erase from her memory.

"That's fine with me. I just thought it'd be good to clear the air." Will jumped up, brushed off his pants and walked over to Justice. He was ready to finish this torture and return to the ranch.

Amanda watched him as he stroked his horse, spoke to him softly, and mounted. She wondered if that was how he treated his women, with soft strokes and calm assurances. Once again Amanda forced her brain to other thoughts, different subjects.

"Have you ever been married, Mr. MacLaren?" As soon as the words were out she wanted to pull them back.

He rested an arm on the horn of his saddle and leaned over Justice's neck so that he could look directly into Amanda's eyes. "Yes." With one quick move he turned Justice and galloped up the hill, toward their next stop.

Amanda hurried to catch up. She felt terrible. It was only one word, but the pain in his eyes was unmistakable. Amanda lagged behind several yards, trying to give him the space she thought he needed. Was his wife still alive, and if so, where was she? Had she died? Are there children?

Will slowed his pace to allow Amanda to catch up since she knew the next location where Jake suspected rustlers had been stealing cattle. Too many head had gone missing from the Big G over the past several months, and if the numbers continued, it would have a significant impact on the profits of the ranch.

"There's a valley up and over that hill, then around to the right, where we often find strays." Amanda rode up alongside Will. "We can almost always count on finding ten or more head there, but lately, nothing. Still, we're losing cattle. It's as if the rustlers know exactly where to look. I can't shake the feeling that someone from the ranch could be feeding information to the thieves."

"How many total are you missing?"

"It's got to be close to a hundred head by now. That's a lot for us." Amanda had not sent word to her father about the cattle. She hated for him to come home to the news but knew if she sent a message he'd only use it as an excuse to shorten the trip and bring her mother home. The trip was important to her mother and Amanda didn't want to be the messenger who ruined it.

"But where do they take them? You don't just hide cattle with ease. Are the other ranchers missing numbers, too?"

"Yes, but not the numbers we are, at least not that I know about. A couple of the ranchers have lost fifteen, twenty head, and Bierdan, at last count, had lost about thirty—at least that's what he told Jake. Got to be over two hundred head by now, including all the ranches. It's not that much total, but it would make a decent profit for someone who hasn't had the expense of raising them."

"Bierdan, you said? Doesn't his land butt up to the Big G?" Will wondered at the coincidence.

"Yes. After us, he's been hit the hardest. He and father started their ranches about the same time, but the two don't get along—never have, from what I can tell. Bierdan doesn't have quite the acreage for grazing. His land is more mountainous, which makes it easier to lose cattle."

"Yet you've lost a lot more. I wonder why that is?" Will's mind raced over the possibility that a neighboring rancher might be somehow involved. Someone who owned a significant amount of mountainous land where it would be easy to separate and hide small herds. He also agreed with Amanda that there could be someone inside the Big G feeding information to the rustlers, but who?

They rode in silence for a while, each lost in their own thoughts. Will rode to a large rock formation and dismounted. Below was the valley Amanda had mentioned and he wanted a better view. It was a dead end, easy for cattle to get lost, and easy for rustlers to move the animals to another location.

"If they grabbed cattle from here, where would they take them? Which direction?"

"Further north would be my guess, away from most of the local ranches. The only one who has more land north is Bierdan, but I don't think he watches it much. Good water, but not much grazing. There's lots of open country up that way—once you get past the mountains—and plenty of long, narrow valleys between the two where the cattle can be hidden. It'd be an easy route to a train station to load the cattle for Denver." Amanda had thought this through so many times that she could almost see the rustlers herding Taylor cattle to market. It was frustrating. She dismounted and joined Will. Exhaustion suddenly overtook her and she dropped to sit against one of the large boulders.

"You all right, Miss Taylor?" Will looked at her with concern. Perhaps they should start back now.

"You know what? I'd really like it if you'd call me Amanda. And, yes, I'm fine, just tired."

He did not want to get on too-friendly-terms with this woman, but her frustration and exhaustion were apparent and he just didn't have it in him to fight her on this one, small point. "If you're sure, Amanda, but you have to call me Will." He dropped down next to her and let his eyes wander over the still-very-pretty but tired features. He was sure he knew the cause. "If it makes you feel better, I didn't sleep last night either."

Her eyes snapped up to his. "I didn't say I didn't sleep..."

"Amanda, we both know what happened last night, and I doubt either of us slept much." He held up his hand at her confused expression. "You're a beautiful woman, and any man would want to have you. Seeing you last night, well, let's just say you were a vision I had a hard time getting out of my head."

"Oh, I see. At least I think I do." She smiled up at him. It was the same smile which first hooked him the day he helped pull the heifer from the mud, and the same smile she threw over her shoulder when she told him good morning. It was like the sun, pouring heat through his body and warming his blood.

Their eyes locked and held. Both tried to hold their ground, but neither could counter the attraction they felt. Almost too slow to notice, they leaned into each other and their lips touched. Soft strokes at first, a leisurely brushing of lips, then more pressure. Will trailed his tongue across her lower lip, coaxing her to open for him. When she did, he reached around and pulled her closer, learning the taste of her, the feel of her pressed against him.

The kiss seemed to go on and on. She'd never been kissed like this before. Her head spun, her senses were in shambles. Her hands moved up his arms to rest on his shoulders. He took control of the kiss only for a minute before she captured his tongue between her lips. The action caused Will to pull her even tighter and deepen the kiss. His hands moved up and down her back, creating heat that radiated through her body.

She let her body mold further to his as her hands crept from his shoulders to encircle his neck. His solid chest felt wonderful against the soft mounds of her breasts, and for the first time in her life she wished she knew how to make love to a man, to this man.

Will couldn't believe what was happening to him. He'd been with other women since Emily, but all had been paid for. They'd served a need. Not one had been a woman he could ever feel anything for, which is how he liked it. No ties, no emotions. But Amanda, he felt things for her he thought he'd never feel again, thought he'd never want to feel again, and certainly didn't want to feel now.

He needed space, to stop whatever was happening between them before she got the idea he'd stay and be here for her. Will knew that wouldn't happen. He ended the kiss and pulled free, looking down into her passion glazed eyes and wishing things could be different.

"We have to stop, Amanda." Will's voice was soft, with none of the hardness she'd become so accustomed to.

She stared up at him, trying to clear her mind. "Yes, of course, you're right. We should start back." She pushed herself up and hurried toward the horses.

"Amanda..."

"We won't speak of this again," she called over her shoulder. She mounted Angel and tried to distance herself from what had just happened. She didn't know how she'd let down her guard and let this man become someone she wanted. The experience back East should have taught her something, but apparently she was just as naïve now as she had been then. At least this time she knew the man she wanted had no intention of staying in Cold Creek. He was as drifter, pure and simple. He'd stay a while, then be gone. It was best this way.

Will knew she was right to ignore the feelings between them, act like they didn't exist, and forget the passion that flared each time they were together. The reason he'd come to Cold Creek had nothing to do with finding someone, building any type of life in Colorado. It was about revenge, and revenge had no place in Amanda's world. Will would finish what needed to be done and ride out, leaving her to find someone else—someone with a clean soul and a clear conscious.

******

"I'll be back as soon as I can, Mr. Dunnigan, but this is something that needs to be done. He can't be left to face it alone." Drew prepared to board the westbound train, toward Cold Creek and his brother. He was certain whatever Will planned included confronting Hawley, killing him, and ending a journey that had already taken five years of his life.

"Believe me, Drew, I understand your need to assist family, but I must also consider the business interests of Dunnigan Enterprises. We've already discussed how this will work for both of us as I don't want to lose you. You've been a valuable addition to the company, and if all goes as it appears, a valuable addition to my family. I'm sure you know Patricia won't be pleased you've left without seeing her, but it has to be done. You take this trip, assist your brother, and look into the business dealings we've discussed. Keep me informed." Louis Dunnigan shook Drew's hand and clapped him on the shoulder. "Good luck to you. Come back as soon as you can."

Drew cringed at the mention of Patricia, Louis Dunnigan's young, beautiful, and very spoiled daughter. A woman who made no secret of her desire to wed the young attorney. But it was a one-sided desire. Drew had no interest in spending his life with a pampered, temperamental female, no matter what wealth she'd bring to a marriage. Besides, Drew knew that eventually he would move back home and take on his responsibilities at the ranch. If he could convince Will to give up his need for revenge and move home, then perhaps Drew would speed up his timing and leave Dunnigan Enterprises sooner than expected.

Dunnigan had always been a fair and honest boss, two traits that were the main reasons Drew stayed. The pay was good and the work challenging, but he understood that some day the pull back to Fire Mountain would cause him to sever his ties with the man.

The train traveled through the majestic peaks between Denver and the western region of Colorado. It followed the same path as the Eagle River and at times, the sides of the mountains appeared to close in, almost trapping those positioned in between. He'd traveled this way before, but only to handle Dunnigan business, nothing as critical as the task before him now. Drew wondered what Will had found to convince him the man who'd killed Emily was still alive and hiding in Cold Creek. The information must be substantial. His brother wasn't one to jump in without considering the consequences of his actions. This time, however, Drew worried about the emotions that would drive Will's actions if he confirmed that Hollis was, in fact, the same man who had murdered Emily. *What would I do if it were me?* Clarity washed through Drew's mind and in an instant he knew exactly what he'd do. The realization surprised him, but made him all the more determined to get to his brother before the MacLarens lost anyone else.

******

"I'm sorry, Torie, but I can't leave Will to face Hawley alone. With my background and skills, I'm the right person to go, and Niall's the best person to stay. The rest of the family will be here for you if the baby comes early." Jamie didn't like leaving his pregnant wife and young son, but Will was in over his head—he just hadn't figured it out yet. "It's something I must do."

"Jamie, it's all right. I'll be fine. Plus, you know that Kate and Aunt Alicia won't let me out of their sight with you gone." Torie understood that her husband needed to leave and supported his decision to go to Colorado. He was right that Will needed him. Jamie's quick mind and fast gun might provide the advantage his brother needed to come out of this with the murderer in jail and Will back home where he belonged.

"I plan to be back in plenty of time before the baby's due, sweetheart, and I don't want you to worry about anything. It'll all work out fine."

Jamie had always been confident in his skills. She'd been on the receiving end of them at one point, and knew first hand how he handled dangerous situations and ruthless killers. "I know it will. Just take care of yourself, and Will, and get home as soon as you can." She smiled into his clear, grey eyes, and tried to memorize them for the long nights ahead. He was the man she'd always loved, and now that they were finally together, she had no wish to lose him to an outlaw's gun.

Chapter Nine

"What's it say, Amanda?" Joey was as anxious for news as everyone else.

"Says they're in New York and will be headed home later this week." She beamed at her brother and felt the excitement of seeing their parents again. "They expect the trip to Cold Creek to take about a week. This is great news."

"What's that you have there, Miss Taylor? Good news I hope."

Oh no, not Chet. "A message from our parents, Mr. Hollis. They're back in the states and will be home real soon." She folded the missive and tucked it in her reticule. "Come on, Joey. I believe we're ready to start home now." She wanted to be as far away from Chet Hollis as possible. The man was a nuisance and refused to take her hints that she had no interest in him whatsoever.

"I'd be honored to take you to dinner, Miss Taylor. Your brother, too."

"Thank you, but that's not necessary. We'll be going now." She turned to leave but the man grabbed her arm to pull her closer to him. "What are you doing, Chet? Let go of me." Her voice rose at the physical intrusion.

"Now, Miss Taylor, Amanda, all I'm asking is to buy you a meal. What's so wrong with that?"

"Because the lady already told you no. Let go of her, now." The hard, raspy voice came from only inches behind Hollis. Chet knew without turning who stood at his back.

Chet dropped his hand from Amanda's arm and spun around to face the one man who still pursued him for the murder in Arizona. He recovered in seconds to plaster a thin smile on his face. "I don't believe I know you, mister. I'm Chet Hollis." Will ignored the extended hand.

"I know who you are, and you already know who I am. We'll meet again, but for now, leave Miss Taylor and Joey alone. Don't ever touch her again. You understand me?" Will's threat was implied but he knew Hollis got the meaning.

"Sure, stranger. I understand you just fine." He tipped his hat to Amanda before walking in the opposite direction, toward the sheriff's office.

Amanda had stood by, listening to the exchange. "You know him, Will?"

"Let's just say I know of him. Keep away from him, Amanda. He's bad news." He continued to watch the killer walk down the dusty boardwalk until he'd disappeared into Dutton's office. Interesting that the first place Hollis would go was the sheriff's office. "If you two are ready, let's grab dinner and head back."

"I'm starved," Joey said and started off toward the hotel restaurant.

Amanda continued to stare at Will, knowing there was much more to the confrontation than he was willing to share. "Thank you for stepping in, but I could've handled the man myself. I've done it many times in the past. You'd think he'd get the message."

Will felt his gut clench at the thought of Hollis anywhere near Amanda, touching her. She was a kind, honest person, and much too trusting to have to confront a lowlife like him. The man needed to be taken care of, and soon.

******

Will rose from the table. "I'll be back in a few minutes, then we'll start for the ranch."

He'd only been gone a short time when Amanda looked up to see him walking towards her but from the front of the restaurant. He'd changed clothes. Everything, including the hat, was different. "Well, that didn't take long," Amanda said as he approached their table.

"Ma'am? Were you speaking to me?" He took off his hat and looked around to see if there was anyone else she might have addressed.

"Very, funny. You changed clothes, but the joke is over now. Let's get going." Amanda started to rise and nodded to Joey to do the same, but Joey just sat, staring at the man with a confused expression.

"Joey?"

"Who are you, Mister?" Joey asked as the man continued to survey the room as if looking for someone.

"His name's MacLaren, Joey, and he's my brother. My twin brother, Drew." Will walked up and clapped Drew on the shoulder, then pulled him in for a hug. "Not that I'm not glad to see you, but what are you doing here? Didn't you get my message?"

"I got it and ignored it." Drew smiled before turning back to the woman and boy who sat with their mouths agape. "Are you going to finish the introductions, Will?"

Will saw the look on his brother's face as his eyes traveled over Amanda. It was not an offensive perusal, but one Will didn't appreciate.

"Amanda, I'd like you to meet my brother, Drew MacLaren. Drew, this is Amanda Taylor. You've already met Joey. I work for their father at the Big G Ranch."

Amanda stared at the image the two men made standing side by side. One brother wore working clothes common to all ranch hands, serviceable clothes that withstood everything from herding cattle to fixing fences—canvas pants and jacket, dark blue striped shirt, scuffed boots, leather gloves tucked into a back pocket, neckerchief, a well-used brown hat, and his side arm.

The second brother wore clothes common to a city life, but not that of a dandy. No, this man was no dandy. Black pants, coat, brocade vest, white shirt, and black tie. She saw the chain of a gold pocket watch before her eyes moved down to see shiny black boots. Her eyes moved back up and she noticed he held a stylish black hat with a small feather in one hand, while the other hand rested on the butt of his Colt Peacemaker. It was the same gun Will used.

"Pleased to meet you, Miss Taylor."

Drew's words pulled her gaze back to his face. Amanda wondered how anyone could tell these two apart if they happened to be wearing the same clothing. "My pleasure, Mr. MacLaren. We didn't know Will had a twin. It's quite remarkable how much alike you are."

"Don't let the looks fool you, Miss Taylor. Other than our looks, we are nothing alike, are we, Will?" The words were for his brother but Drew's eyes never left Amanda.

"No, Drew, we are nothing alike. At least not anymore." Will couldn't hide the sadness in his voice.

Drew's eyes snapped from Amanda to Will at the tone in his brother's voice. He spoke the truth when he stated they were no longer anything alike, but Drew knew it was more than just their personalities––so much more.

"Amanda, would you mind getting back to the ranch on your own?" Will needed to spend time with Drew, get to the truth of his arrival in Cold Creek.

"No, of course not." Her gaze shifted to Drew. "Mr. MacLaren, we'll expect you tonight for supper, and you'll be staying at the ranch. A brother of Will's won't be staying in the local hotel. Joey, let's get going." Amanda wasted not another word but walked out with Joey right behind.

"Not your typical invitation, but then I'm guessing she's not typical in a lot of ways." Drew smiled at the woman's departing back.

"No, not typical at all. Come on, I'll buy you a drink and you can explain to me what the hell you're doing here."

******

"Tess, you're back!" Amanda jumped off the wagon and ran to her closest friend, Tessa Kelly, giving her a warm hug. "I expected you back a week ago."

"Me too, but Uncle Joe and Aunt Mary insisted I stay until my cousins could visit. They've all changed so much I'm glad I stayed, but happy to be home." Tessa turned to see Joey standing a few feet away. "Well, Sir Joey, don't I get a hug from my best man?"

"Hey, Tess." Joey ran up to wrap his arms around her waist.

The three had always been close, more like siblings than friends. Tessa was about two years younger than Amanda, and like her friend, had been born on the ranch. Her father, Robert—or Bobby, as the ranch hands called him—had held the chief wrangler job until he died when Tess was thirteen. A fever had taken her mother a year later and she'd lived with the Taylor's ever since. She could

84

ride as well as Amanda, and knew how to run a household, a skill Eleanor Taylor required of both young ladies, but her real love had always centered on two things—horses and books. Her dream was to breed the best ranch horses in Colorado and Grant Taylor had always encouraged her.

"Oh, Amanda, you should've seen the library in Chicago. I've never been in such a magnificent building. There were rows of books on ranching and horses, and Uncle Joe and Aunt Mary allowed me to visit it several times." Tess beamed as she spoke of her time spent researching breeds, lineage, and how best to produce the type of horses she saw as the future of the Big G. She grabbed Amanda's arm and walked with her into the house as she continued on about the wonders of Chicago. "Okay, enough about my trip. What's been happening here since I left?"

"Not much. Same old stuff that always happens on the ranch."

"We got a new ranch hand, and Amanda's sweet on him." Joey threw this out just before he took off toward the barn so as to miss his sister's reaction.

"What? Is that true, Amanda?"

Amanda continued to glare at her brother's departing back while she answered. "No, it certainly is not true. We do have a new ranch hand but I am not sweet on him or anyone else."

"Well, tell me about him." Unlike Amanda, Tess had never been courted. She'd never seemed to care one way or the other about men, settling down, or raising a family. She wasn't confortable speaking with men, or anyone, for that matter, other than her close friends and family. Tess had always been more focused on her dream of horse breeding.

"Not much to tell. Name's Will MacLaren and he's a good hand. Knows his trade, works hard, and keeps to himself. Oh yes, and he has a twin brother who showed up in town today. Pretty unexpected, judging by Will's reaction. I invited him to supper and to stay at the ranch while he's in Cold Creek. He makes quite an impression." Amanda smiled. She'd been impressed with Drew's appearance but what had caught her attention was the obvious fact that he'd been well educated. "Let's let Maria know you're back and we're having a guest. We'll get you unpacked so you have time to rest before supper. We've got so much more to talk about."

******

"You're telling me Jamie's on his way here, too? Hell, Drew, why don't Niall, Sam Browning, and Trent Garner come along also? Might as well have all the men here in Cold Creek for a battle I can handle on my own." Will slammed the whiskey back before pouring another. He couldn't help the disgusted tone. His family was interfering and he'd have none of it.

Drew knew his brother too well to be dragged into the muck on this one. There were reasons the family had decided to come to Cold Creek, good ones, and they all centered on keeping Will alive and stop him from breaking the law in his quest for vengeance. "Tough thing for a man to have family who cares about him, right, Will?" Drew sipped his drink while he waited for his twin's reaction.

"Hell, Drew, don't start that shit. I love them, you know that. But this is my fight, not yours or theirs."

"Your fight is our fight, Will. Can you understand that? If the man who killed Emily is here in Cold Creek, let us help you. Don't do this alone."

"And if one of you is killed, hurt, how do you think I'll feel?" Will took another swallow of whiskey while watching the saloon doors. He didn't want anyone to know his brother had arrived. No sense making him a target. "No, Drew, this is my fight to win or lose."

Drew studied his brother for several long moments, trying to determine how far he could be pushed without shutting down. That had become his normal method of dealing with conversations he didn't want to face. He'd let Will retreat for now, but the discussion, and the family's involvement, were far from settled.

"I'm hungry. What time is supper at the ranch?" Drew finished his drink, signaling he'd also finished talking, for now.

"Fine, we'll ride out now, but I'm telling you, I don't want anyone else I care about involved. I have no intention of losing any more of my family."

******

"I swear to you, Chet, the man looks just like Will MacLaren, but all gussied up. Rode in today and went straight to the restaurant next to the hotel. After awhile Miss Taylor and Joey came out and took off home, then MacLaren and the stranger walked to the saloon. Got to be brothers, maybe twins." Sheriff Dutton had sought out Hollis soon after watching the happenings with MacLaren.

"So what? Doesn't mean anything to us. We just keep doing what we planned and everything will work out fine." Chet had stayed in town after his run-in with MacLaren, gotten supplies, and landed in the saloon not long after Will and Drew left for the Big G. This was his second trip to Dutton's office that day. He'd been ready to leave the saloon and ride out when the sheriff signaled that he needed to speak with him.

"You're just not understanding this. The man wore a gun, same as MacLaren. We already know he has a brother that was a marshal, a real mean bastard. Now another brother shows up. I don't like it, not one bit."

Chet pondered this awhile, sipped his whiskey, and leaned back in his chair. "The boss wants more cattle. He's not satisfied with the count, and isn't going to be until we give him what he wants. I've already spoken to our contact at the Taylor ranch and he's ready to move whenever I give the word. He feels he can handle MacLaren, and we can handle the stranger, if it comes to it. You just find out who this stranger is, determine if he's connected to MacLaren. I'll go out to speak with the rest of the men, give them warning that we may need to move quick. As long as we don't panic, we'll be okay."

Dutton wasn't convinced. He knew Jamie MacLaren, and if he showed up, the sheriff already planned to take off without a backward glance. He wasn't going to fight a battle he knew they'd lose over a few head of cows. "I'll find out what I can on the stranger, but you just heed what I said. These MacLarens aren't men you want to mess with."

Chapter Ten

"How'd you end up in Denver, Drew?" Amanda looked across the table at their guest. He'd shared little about himself. At least she'd learned there were two more brothers—Niall, the oldest and head of the MacLaren clan, and Jamie, the second oldest and an ex-marshal. She wondered if they were as handsome as the two at her table.

"Luck, actually. A client at the New York office wanted someone to head up the Denver operations, expand the cattle part of their business. The combination of my law degree and ranching background made sense. I volunteered. It's been over a year but I'm about ready to move on, go back home."

Will shot a look towards Drew at the last statement. It was the first time he'd heard Drew mention going home, back to the ranch and their family. A strange sensation slashed through his heart, but disappeared just as quickly.

"If you don't mind me asking, is that what brought you to Cold Creek? Are you on your way back home?" Tessa had spoken little during the meal. She preferred to listen and not join the conversation when guests were present. But this stranger intrigued her. He'd had extensive education, and like her, he loved books and learning. But he also loved ranching.

"No. I knew Will was here and thought it'd be a good time to see him. Not a long journey from

Denver, and I'd wanted to visit the western part of the state for some time." Drew sipped coffee as Amanda passed around the cake Maria had made. "Seems like a peaceful town, from what I've seen so far."

"Well, first impressions aren't always accurate. There's a lot going on, making life difficult on all the ranchers, not just here at the Big G. We're hoping it'll all settle down when our parents return next week. Right, Jake?" Amanda looked at their foreman, hoping he'd enter the conversation, but he continued to sit in silence, preferring to size up the stranger in his own way. "Father will take care of the problems. I'm sure of it."

"What problems?" Drew asked.

"Cattle rustling, accidents with no explanation," Will said. "Losses have hit the Big G the hardest, but several places have lost a part of their herd." Will leaned forward. "Amanda showed me the places where cattle have gone missing. Only Big G ranch hands know where cattle will be pastured, and that information is provided to them by Jake on the day they move the cattle. It's only been a few days since Amanda and Jake made the connection, but within a day or two of being moved, some of the cattle are missing. Just makes sense that someone here is passing on information about grazing locations."

"Do the same hands move the cattle each time, or do you rotate duties?" Drew directed his question to Jake.

"Been rotating for the most part, but at least three men are always included in the group. Known two of them for years, Tinder and Mullins, but the third only a couple of months. Came recommended, but something's never seemed quite right about him."

"Who recommended him?" Drew asked.

"One of the hands at the Bierdan place, Del Wiley. Guess the two worked together down in New Mexico."

Will's senses went on alert at the mention of Chet Hollis's friend. He doubted it was a coincidence but said nothing. "What's the man's name?"

"Alts. Frank Alts. You've worked with him a couple of times now, Will."

Will had worked with him but felt the same as Jake. Something just wasn't quite right with Alts, but he had yet to figure out what. "Yea, a couple of times. Sticks close, but doesn't say much."

"Alts? Now why does that name sound familiar?" Drew looked at Will.

"I thought the same, but nothing about him is familiar. Maybe he came through Fire Mountain at some point, worked at one of the ranches," Will responded.

"Don't matter," Jake said. "I've decided I'm going to have Will be part of the group. He can keep an eye on Alts and the others."

"Yea? And how do you know I'm not part of it?" His eyes focused on Jake. There was no humor in Will's voice.

"Son, I've known a lot of ranch hands, good and bad. Now, I'm not saying I know everything about you, but you're no mere wrangler. You're a rancher, plain and simple. You'd no more rustle cattle than you'd take up with a married woman."

The room fell silent for an instant before Drew's deep laugh broke the calm. "He's got you there, brother." Drew slapped Will on the back. Jake was right. Will wouldn't steal, cheat, or lie to get what he wanted, and he'd never take up with another man's wife.

Amanda and Tessa glanced at each other across the table. Jake hadn't shared his thoughts on Will with Amanda before, but now all she'd witnessed seem to click into place. There was much more to Will MacLaren than he wanted anyone to see.

"Just where did you learn to ranch, Will?" Amanda tried to keep the intense curiosity from her voice, but she was eager to learn more about this very private man. She realized that despite her best intentions, her feelings for Will grew each day, and she was determined to find a reason to push those feelings aside, bury them. Her only other experience with a man had been a disaster and she had no wish to repeat it with a wandering cowboy.

"Our uncle's ranch in Arizona. He took us in when our folks died. Been in it most of our lives," Drew responded when it became obvious that Will wasn't going to. "We," he nodded at his twin, "were seven, and I still remember my first sight of a large herd of cattle and a couple dozen cowboys. When Uncle Stuart died, the ranch passed to us and our Aunt Alicia."

Will sat listening, remembering that only a few short years ago it would've been him pulling people into the conversation, with Drew sitting on the sidelines. He'd joke and laugh while Drew would listen, absorb the personalities, and ask

93

pointed questions. There were days Will didn't recognize the man he'd become, or remember the one he'd been.

"You said you're from Fire Mountain?" Jake asked. When Drew nodded, he continued. "Ever hear of a guy named Josh Jacklin? Good hand. Thought I heard he ended up near there."

"Sure have. He's the foreman at a ranch next to ours. Works for a man we've known most of our lives, Trent Garner. Both are very good men." Again it was Drew who spoke.

"Will, if you have such a large, successful cattle ranch in Arizona, why are you here? Seems like you'd be working your own ranch, with your family." This time it was Tess who spoke up—curiosity over-riding her usual shyness.

"I've got my reasons." Will pushed up from the table and nodded at the ladies. "If you'll excuse me, tomorrow's going to be a long day."

Amanda watched his retreating back and wondered again how she could be developing feelings for such a private, closed man. "Well, gentlemen, if you'll excuse Tessa and me. She's had a long day of travel and I've some book work I need to finish. Leave the dishes. Maria will be out to put everything away. Drew, it is so good to have you here. We'll see you at breakfast." Amanda and Tessa excused themselves and the men made their way outside. Jake headed to the bunkhouse while Drew walked toward the barn. He knew Will would be inside, calming himself the same way he'd always done, by grooming Justice.

"Del Wiley? Isn't that the man you said is friends with Chet Hollis?" Drew asked as he strolled up to his brother.

"Yea, and I don't like coincidences. It seems odd the Taylor's would start missing cattle about the time Wiley's other friend, Alts, was hired by Jake. Nothing adds up. Sure wish I could remember where I've heard that name before. Somehow I think it's important I figure it out."

"What about the other men Jake mentioned, Tinder and Mullins? Any thoughts on them?"

"Tinder's safe enough, except the boy has it bad for Amanda." Will shook his head, stood, and threw the brush in a bucket with the others. The disgusted tone of his voice wasn't lost on his brother. "Don't know much about Mullins. Both are younger than Alts, but hang on every word the man says. Could be a bad sign if Alts is involved in the thefts."

"Men that steal aren't too averse to pulling good men into their plans, then letting them take the blame. Better keep an eye on all three. What do you want me to do?" Drew asked.

"Go home, back to Denver or to Arizona. Just get out of here, Drew. I don't need to worry about anyone while I work this out with Hollis." Will's voice had turned hard, harder than Drew expected given that he'd already made it clear he wasn't leaving.

"Not happening. You'll just have to get used to having me around for a while. Now, what can I do?" They were the same height, six-feet-three-inches, and stood eye-to-eye, not a foot apart.

Drew's eyes bored into Will's. He'd not leave his brother to fight Hollis alone.

Will knew he couldn't force Drew to leave, short of a fight. They'd only gone head-to-head one time in their lives, and that was when they were seventeen, and both smitten with the same girl—— a girl who later became Will's wife, Emily. No, he wouldn't fight his brother this time.

He broke eye contact and made the decision to take advantage of the offer to help. "All right, if that's the way it's going to be, I'd appreciate it if you'd talk to Sheriff Dutton. He knows Hollis, but I believe he knows a lot more than he lets on. Be careful, I don't trust the sheriff, nor anyone associated with him."

"No problem. I'll ride into town tomorrow and snoop around. Nothing I like better than a good puzzle." Drew smiled and turned back toward the house, and bed.

******

"I'm telling you, Chet, those MacLaren boys know more than you think." Frank Alts had overheard Will and Drew outside the barn the night before. He'd ridden in late after checking on a herd from a neighboring ranch and just happened to catch their conversation. Chet planned to raid the rancher's cattle and merge them with the others he'd stolen over the past three months, but Alts wanted no part of the plan that might blow-up now that the MacLarens were poking around.

Frank's reasons for not wanting the MacLarens in the way were his own. He wouldn't share them with Hollis or anyone else. "We need to move the herd tomorrow or hold off. Any longer and they may figure out what's going on."

"Calm down, Frank. You're getting as bad as Dutton regarding MacLaren. The man can't tie any of us to the missing cattle." Hollis stopped to consider Alt's plan to move the cattle the following night. "But you may be right about moving the herd tomorrow. Let's go with your idea. I'll notify the others later today." He stopped Alts as he turned to leave. "And, Frank, don't go getting any second thoughts on our deal. No one walks out on me. You understand?"

Alts stared at Chet. He could get rid of the man at any time, but that wasn't his goal. Chet thought Frank wanted quick money and a clean escape but there was much more to his being involved with a man like Hollis. He'd kill Chet without a second thought if it was needed, but it wasn't going to happen, at least not tonight.

"Sure, Chet. I understand." Alts walked away, his mind racing with what he knew and the need to contact his partner. Unfortunately, his partner hadn't showed up for their last meeting and Frank had no way to reach him short of leaving Cold Creek. The arrival of not one, but two MacLarens, complicated everything that had been so carefully planned. He needed to concentrate on what he knew and how to proceed. Most important, he had to find a way to make sure no one got killed in what had become a very dangerous game.

Chapter Eleven

"Jake, where's Alts? I haven't seen him since he rode in this afternoon, and he didn't show for supper." Will walked up to the foreman who was making his way from the main house to the stables.

"Don't know where he is. Why?"

"Something doesn't seem right, is all. He rode in, grabbed more gear, muttered something about getting cows out of trouble, and took off again. Mullins rode out a short time later, but Tinder's still here, and says he doesn't know where they went."

"Which way?" Jake asked.

"North. Don't you have a small herd up that direction?"

"Sure do, but we also have our remuda up in that area in a fenced pasture. Only two people know the location of those extra horses––Amanda and me. Problem is, they're not far from the cattle, and just as valuable. Maybe more. Get your brother," Jake called over his shoulder as he walked toward his horse and gear.

"Drew, outside, now." Eyes snapped up at Will's harsh tone. He'd walked in on an unexpected scene, his brother sitting almost head to head with Amanda, whispering, and looking down into their almost joined laps. "What's going on here?"

"Look, Will." Amanda's words were soft and the blazing smile she offered made him wince at his poor behavior. "Kittens."

"Kittens? We may be losing cattle and horses, and you two are crooning over kittens?"

"What're you talking about?" Drew stood to face his brother.

"Grab your horse. You, Jake, and I are riding north. We think Alts and Mullins are up there trying to steal the cattle, and maybe the remuda. We need to be sure both are protected."

"Wait. I'm going with you..." Amanda started before being cut off by both men.

"No!" Will and Drew answered in unison.

"Yes, I am. This is my ranch and I won't be left behind." Amanda dashed up the stairs, leaving the brothers to stare after her.

"Now what?" Drew asked.

"Hell, I don't know. Wait, I guess. Unless Jake tells her to stay behind we don't have a choice." Unless Jake interceded, Will was already resigned to Amanda riding along. Now there'd be one more person to protect.

"You boys coming or not?" Jake had grown tired of waiting.

"It's Amanda. She insists on coming along," Drew said.

"Ah, hell," Jake grumbled but looked as resigned to the situation as Will did.

Drew empathized with both men, but shook it off. "Come on, Will. I could use some help with the horses."

"Jake, you mind helping Drew? I want to speak with Amanda before we leave." Will's voice was somber but Drew could sense the tension building.

"Let's go, Drew," Jake said as he walked out the door.

Will looked up as he heard Amanda's boots on the stairs. "You didn't have to wait," Amanda said as she walked into the room.

"We need to talk."

"Can't it wait, Will?"

"No, now."

Amanda was used to Will being in control, in charge. He was good at hiding his emotions, but not now. She'd never seen him uncomfortable—as if he needed to deliver a message he wished could remain unsaid.

"I'm asking you to not come along, Amanda. Stay here, where you'll be safe." Will's voice was almost a plea, not just a request, and his concern obvious.

"Why would I stay here, when someone may be trying to steal our cattle? I don't understand how you could ask me this."

"Because there could be shooting. Someone could get killed. I don't want that to be you. Can you understand?" Will had no other words for the dread he felt at her joining them.

"I understand that you feel responsible for my safety, but you're not. Only I can decide what I need to do. Thank you for your concern, but I'm coming with you." Amanda wouldn't budge. Her parents had left her in charge and she wouldn't let them down.

Will's dread increased with each word she spoke. Someone was going to get hurt tonight, he felt it, and could only hope it wouldn't be Amanda. "All right, but stay with me." When she began to balk at his command, Will continued, his voice strained. "I mean it, Amanda. If you don't stay with me and do as I say, I'll tie you to my horse so I know where you are. You got that?"

"You wouldn't."

"Don't test me. I wouldn't say it if I wasn't prepared to do it."

The two stared at each other before a shout from Drew brought them back to the present. "You two coming?"

Without another word, Amanda turned and stomped outside, mounted her horse, and nudged Angel into a gallop that had her out of sight within a minute.

"Damn, Will. What did you say to get her so riled up?" Jake asked.

"I told her I'd tie her to Justice if she didn't stay with me when we got to the valley."

"Ah, well, can't imagine why that would set her off." Jake cast a look at Drew before following the woman at a safe distance.

******

"What do you see, Drew?" Will looked up at his brother who'd climbed a small rock formation to get a better look into the valley

101

used for the extra horses. Jake was perched beside him. According to Jake, the remuda had been in this location about a week, but until tonight, only he and Amanda had known the location. At least that's what they'd thought.

"Nothing except the horses. I count fifteen. Is that right, Jake?"

"That'd be right. Looks like they haven't found this location or just haven't arrived."

"How far to the cattle?" Will asked.

"About two miles, so we'd better start riding." Jake was anxious to find the people responsible for the thefts. His gut told him they were close.

Drew and Jake began their descent but looked up at the sound of approaching horses.

"Well, what have we here?" Drew asked no one in particular as he looked down on four riders approaching the remuda. "We've got four men surrounding the horses. Jake, see if you can make out who they are."

"Looks like Alts and Mullins, but I don't recognize the other two. Do you, Will?" Jake worked to control his anger at finding two of his hands robbing the Big G. He'd never tolerated a thief, but it was worse when it was your own men.

Will climbed up beside the others and peered over the rocks. "No. Here's what we'll do. Drew, you head around left. Jake, you go right, and I'll head straight in."

"Which direction should I go?" Amanda prepared herself for the anticipated response.

"You'll stay here, make sure no one gets past us. We can't afford to have one of them ride out and warn the rest of the group. Can you do that?"

She couldn't contain her smile. She'd been prepared to fight Will, ride in with them even if he ordered her away. "Yes, I can handle it."

"Good. Let's go."

Amanda ground tied her horse, grabbed her rifle, and walked toward a small knoll with a good view of the meadow and remuda. A rider could get over the rocky terrain across from her, but it would take time. The outlaws would choose the shortest route, which meant they'd ride right past her for a quick escape. She settled in and watched Will, Jake, and Drew ride forward and take positions that would allow them to move in without being seen. There wasn't much cover, but the noise from the horses, and a new moon, which cast no light, helped hide their approach.

It happened fast.

Will dismounted, slid behind a nearby rock, and aimed his rifle at one of the men he didn't recognize. "Hold up, gentlemen. You're not leaving with those horses." His voice carried through the small pasture and over the noise of the horses, but seemed to have no impact on the four men.

First Alts, then Mullins and the others, raised their heads when they heard the warning. Instead of heeding it, they all went for their weapons and turned towards the voice. One of the men Jake hadn't recognized fired first, his shot wild, hitting rocks above Will's head. Mullins got one shot off toward Drew's location, but missed.

A shot from Will disabled the closest man with a clean hit through his right shoulder. No sooner had the man slumped in his saddle than the other three spun their horses around and continued to shoot into the sightless night. Drew aimed at the one closest to his position. The man hit the ground at the same instant the remaining two rode straight toward the canyon entrance, leaving their comrades and horses behind.

"Pull up!" Will ordered. The two rode straight toward him and their escape. The only answer was several shots that ricocheted off the ground and rock. Will's next three shots missed as he tried, without success, to slow the retreating riders. It was up to Amanda.

Behind a small boulder, Amanda steadied her rifle. She watched as the two riders approached, both huddled low in their saddles. One shot rang out as she squeezed the trigger. One of the outlaws fell. As she sighted in on the fourth man, a bullet hit the ground next to her, spewing up rock and dirt. Amanda dropped back behind the boulder, mentally deriding herself for not getting a second shot off sooner. Then reality hit. Her stomach clenched as her body began to shake. She'd shot a man. *Is he dead?* The rifle fell from her hands. At the sound of loud voices, she looked up and around the boulder to see

Will and Jake kneeling next to the man she'd shot. Without thought she raced toward them, fell to the ground, and stared into familiar eyes. Johnny Mullins.

Tears formed in her eyes as she frantically tried ripping some cloth from her skirt to stop his bleeding.

"It's no use, Amanda. He's not going to make it." Will put a hand on her shoulder, but she shook it off and tried to work faster.

"Johnny? Johnny, can you hear me?" Amanda leaned in close and gently pushed hair off the dying man's forehead. "Johnny, talk to me."

His glazed eyes opened just enough to recognize the woman kneeling over him. A slight frown formed on his face. He winced and coughed up blood.

"I'm sorry, Miss Amanda." He coughed again and his face contorted with pain. "I shouldn't have gone with him. Shouldn't have gone." That was all he got out before his eyes lost their sight and his breathing ceased.

"Oh no, Johnny. What have I done?" Amanda's anguished voiced sliced through Will. This time she didn't resist as he pulled her close.

"It's not your fault, Amanda. He tried to steal the horses. You stopped him. It was the only thing you could do." Will stared into grief-stricken eyes and tightened his hold on her.

"I'll take care of him, Will. You get Amanda to her horse." Jake held a blanket and knelt to cover the dead man's body.

Will nodded as he guided Amanda away. He understood the gut-wrenching feeling of killing someone. The first time was the worst and he knew the scene would haunt Amanda for a long time. Hopefully, she'd never experience it again. But they lived in a land populated by men who had no qualms about stealing. And killing.

"It's not your fault." Will repeated his earlier statement. This time Amanda lifted her head and nodded slightly.

"I know." Amanda's voice was flat. At his doubtful stare, she continued. "And I'll be fine. Really. But I don't understand why. Why would he do this?"

"Only Johnny knew why he got involved in something like this." Will couldn't focus on the dead man. "Right now we have a bigger problem. Jake recognized the rider who rode off. Alts, which means he won't go back to the ranch. We'll take the horses back with us tonight then split them into smaller groups at the ranch. It won't be safe to pasture them too far away. The loss of the full remuda would set you back a good deal of money as well as time." Will looked off over the hills beyond. This was a complication he didn't need. His focus should be on Hollis, not some group of rustlers stealing horses and cattle from people who meant nothing to him. No, this was not his fight.

"If you two are ready, we need to get started." Drew had ridden up without either noticing. "The three dead are tied to their horses and strung together. Amanda? Are you okay leading them back to the ranch while Jake, Will, and I handle the remuda?"

"Sure, Drew. I'll get Angel." Amanda walked off to find her horse grazing not far away. She wondered how Tinder would take the news about Johnny. They'd been close, basically inseparable, as Jake had commented more than once. The thought stopped her. Could Tinder be involved, or know what his friend was doing? Amanda didn't want to think about how not only Johnny, but possibly Tinder, could've fooled so many people.

Chapter Twelve

Amanda was tired and discouraged by the time she spotted the big ranch house around the last bend. She rode past the barn and guided the three horses into a corral. She untied the lead rope to each horse but left the dead bodies as they were. She'd leave that job to the others.

"Good Lord, Amanda, what happened?" Tess ran to her friend as soon as she heard the approach of horses. Surveying the scene she stared in disbelief at the body of the one she recognized. Johnny Mullins. When her friend didn't respond, Tess turned and wrapped her hand around Amanda's upper arm. "Amanda, tell me what happened out there."

Before Amanda could reply they heard the sound of horses and turned to see Jake, Will, and Drew guiding the remuda into the largest corral. Drew jumped down to secure the gate as Jake and Will made their way to where the women stood.

"I suppose Amanda told you what happened," Jake said to Tess.

"No, she hasn't said a word," Tess kept her eyes on Amanda. She had never seen her friend look this grim.

"Will, can you and Drew handle things here? Send a couple of men into town with the bodies. They should notify the sheriff, even though I expect he won't do a thing about it. I'll take Tess inside and explain. Come on, Amanda, you too." Jake felt responsible for Amanda coming along and dreaded the encounter with her parents when they arrived back at the ranch.

"No, Jake. I'll stay and help. I need to do this." Amanda's words were directed at her foreman but her eyes stared at Johnny's body, still tied to his horse.

Jake started to reply, but a glance from Will stopped him.

Tess looked from Will to Amanda, then back to Jake. "Let's go inside. I'll make coffee for everyone, and you need to get that leg up." Tess scanned Amanda's face once more, then turned to walk the short distance to the house.

"You don't have to do this, Amanda. Drew and I can handle it. It'd be better if you weren't here." Will knew his voice sounded hard, harder than intended, but he didn't want her handling the bodies, reliving the scene.

Amanda raised her chin, eyes flashing, and seemed to draw strength from the challenge Will threw at her. "It's my family's ranch, Will. It was my bullet that killed Johnny. You can go inside if you like, but I'm staying here. Do we understand each other?"

Will's eyes narrowed to slits. He stared at her for a long moment. "Yes, ma'am, I believe we do. Drew and I will stay. Get this done quick." He glanced at his twin who'd walked up but stood silent.

"Why don't you get a wagon ready, Amanda? We'll load the bodies for the trip to town." Drew said.

Both men walked past Amanda into the corral and began to untie the dead men, letting the bodies slide to the ground. Within minutes Will and Drew had unsaddled the three horses and had carried the bodies outside the corral.

Amanda pulled up in the wagon as the men approached with Johnny.

"What's going on?" It was Tinder, jogging out of the bunkhouse with several men following. He stopped and stared at the body they carried. "Johnny? What the hell happened?" he choked out before he turned to the side and gagged.

Amanda's heart twisted at the pain she saw in Tinder's face. "I did it, Tinder. It was me. I shot him." She looked directly at the ranch hand, waiting.

"You? But why?" Tinder was dumbstruck, not only at the death of his friend, but at the confession of the woman before him.

Drew explained. "Johnny was with Alts and two other men who were attempting to steal the remuda. They pulled guns and started to ride off. There was no choice, Tinder. Amanda's shot hit Johnny." Will and Amanda watched the reactions of the other ranch hands.

"And Alts?" A tall, older man spoke from the back of the group.

"We didn't get him. He rode off, probably to catch up with the group he's working with. We're going to be talking to each one of you, find out if you know anything about Alts that would help us find him," Drew said.

Will looked over the men again and wondered which ones, if any, might be involved with Alts in the thefts. "Caldwell, Hutchins, load the other two bodies, then take the wagon into town and bring back the sheriff, if he'll come." The two men nodded. He turned his attention to the others. "Like Drew said, we'll need to speak with each of you. Tinder, I want you to go with Drew, inside to the office, get some coffee. Amanda and I'll join you in a few minutes."

"I had nothing to do with this, if that's what you're thinking," Tinder began to protest, but Will held up a hand to stop him.

"We're not accusing anyone. You're the first because you and Johnny were friends and you worked with Alts more than the others. You might have heard or seen something that could help. That's it." Will looked at the others. "The rest of you go on back to the bunkhouse for now." He turned to Amanda. "I figured you'd want to be there when we talk with Tinder."

"Jake should be there, too. He hired most of the men and knows Tinder better than the rest of us. I'll meet you in the house." Amanda trudged up the steps and into the house without another glance at anyone. What she wanted was to wash up, climb into bed, and sleep. What she needed to do was the same thing her father would if he were here——meet with the men and find out as much as possible before any of them decided to take off. She headed for the kitchen.

"How are you doing?" Tess was at the sink rinsing cups and preparing more coffee. She knew Amanda was excellent with a gun, but had never shot at anyone before. Tess realized the extent that Johnny's death hurt her friend, even if she didn't want everyone else to see it. Amanda had always been strong, people relied on her, but even the strongest person could only shoulder so much. "Can I do anything for you? Get you something?"

"No, thanks. I just want to clean up before meeting with Tinder and the others in Father's office." Amanda ran a hand through her hair and took a deep, ragged breath. "I didn't know it was Johnny until he was down. It doesn't make sense, Tess. He loved it here. Always talked about learning everything he could so he could be a foreman somewhere in the future." Her confused eyes found her friend's then slid to the ground.

"The way Jake tells it, you didn't have a choice, Amanda. Johnny was part of the group, shooting the same as everyone else, and trying to get away. Jake would've done the same, so would Will and Drew. Johnny made his choice. Maybe someday we'll learn why." Tess put an arm around Amanda, pulling her close.

"I know you're right, but it feels horrible just the same. Nothing will ever remove the picture from my head of Johnny on the ground, bleeding and looking up at me." Amanda walked over to the sink and grabbed a glass for water. It was time to meet the others. "I'll be up late. Don't wait as this could take a while. We'll talk in the morning."

******

"What do you mean, they killed the others?" Hollis stomped towards Alts and grabbed the man's shirt until they were nose-to-nose. "What the hell happened?"

"Don't know what happened. But Jake and the new man, MacLaren, were waiting for us. A couple of others, too, but I didn't see them. One was probably MacLaren's brother." Alts shoved Hollis away and stepped back. The man was a loose cannon. Alts rested his hand on the butt of his gun. "Someone must've tipped them off, but I don't know who. No one else at the Big G knows what's been going on, unless you have another pair of eyes on the place and haven't told me." There wasn't any mistaking the accusatory tone in Alts' voice. He didn't trust Hollis. Alts knew the man was pure evil and wondered again how much longer he could endure his association with such a snake. "There's something else. Johnny Mullins saw me ride out and followed along. Thought we were just going to check the cattle, and no matter what I said he refused to head back. He's dead."

"So they believe he was with you to take the horses? Stupid fool. He would've ended up dead either way, as he'd never have gone along with stealing from the Big G. The kid would've turned you in, and the rest of us, too." Hollis paced the small space in the old cabin where they always met. It was a few miles north of the Big G and Bierdan ranches, and most thought it deserted.

"Well, they know that I'm involved. We need to move the cattle we've already taken and get out of here. It's not safe to stick around." Alts spit the words out.

"Like I've said, I'm not ready to close up and neither is the boss. My plans don't include running. Don't underestimate me, Frank. I'll get what I want and no one, including you, will stop me." He turned his back on Alts to look out a window.

Alts listened but ignored the threat. He knew Sheriff Dutton had been trying without success to talk Hollis into taking what they'd already stolen and leave the area, especially now that Will MacLaren had trailed Hollis to Cold Creek. Hollis didn't know it, but Frank Alts knew exactly who he really was––Chad Hawley––and he knew that Chad had murdered MacLaren's wife. Hollis was one of the few men that Alts would never underestimate. Another was Will MacLaren, or any of his brothers.

"None of us signed up for this, Hollis. It was to be a couple of quick raids and leave. We can't stay now. It's too risky for everyone."

Hollis turned back at Alts' comment and aimed his revolver at the man's chest. "I don't need a coward in the group, Frank. Besides, it seems to me you're the only link tying me and the rest of the boys to the raids."

Alts moved quickly, but not fast enough to pull his gun or dodge the shot from only ten feet away. He felt the pain seconds after his wide, surprised eyes locked on Hollis. He grabbed his chest and slowly sank to the ground. His last thoughts were of his young son before darkness took him. Who would take care of Aaron?

Chapter Thirteen

"What do you think, Jake? Is Tinder in on it?" Will's exhausted voice filtered through the night air as the three men walked outside after the last ranch hand had disappeared into the bunkhouse. Amanda had stayed behind with the men for a short time to sort through what they'd learned, but had finally gone upstairs, leaving the brothers and Jake to themselves.

"Don't know for sure but it appears to me he's telling the truth and the other hands don't seem to know anything, either. Tinder and Mullins spent most all their time working together——hardly saw one without the other." The foreman stopped a moment as if to compose his thoughts. "Appears that Mullins couldn't sleep and took a ride. Must've run into Alts. After that, only Alts knows what happened, and if Mullins was involved or not. I sure hope he was as I don't know how Amanda will take it if she learns he was just an innocent."

"She sure seems to be handling it well for someone who's never shot a man before. But it's got to be tough. Never a good thing, to kill someone," Drew commented.

"I've known that girl her whole life. She's stronger than most think. Amanda can handle this and be stronger for it." Jake didn't mention how much inner turmoil he thought she'd endure before reconciling herself to the fact a man was dead at her hand. She'd hide it from most people, but he and Tess would know.

"We need to find Alts. He's the only one who knows the truth and where to find the missing cattle. And the man's not working alone. The ones we killed are only a few of the men involved. Wouldn't surprise me if one man planned it all but hired the others to carry out the thefts." Will had heard of similar patterns before. This was too big to be carried out by a handful of rustlers.

"I've seen this at the large cattle ranches near Denver. Gangs stay around an area long enough to gather a significant number of cattle from several ranches. Hole them up someplace until they can change the brands and be driven to market." Drew paused to take a sip from his now cold coffee. "They're not looking for ten or twenty head, but several hundred. The man we're looking for wouldn't be a part of any raid. He'd stay in the background and organize the details––where to keep the cattle, who to hire, how to get them out of the area. He'd be coldblooded. Wouldn't take any dissention from his men, and he'd be prepared to kill if needed. Might not do the killing himself, but he'd have no issues with ordering it done. And he'd hire a lead man just like him—ruthless. These men are in it for high dollars and power. It's a world most don't know exists."

"How do you know about all this?" Jake asked.

"My boss in Denver, Louis Dunnigan, owns large cattle operations and has dealt with this type of thing before. It can get real ugly." Drew threw out the last of his cold brew and rested against the side of the house. He was tired and wanted nothing more than to head inside to his bed.

"What'd he do to stop it and find the men responsible?" Will asked.

"Understand, Dunnigan is as hardnosed as the men who try to steal from him. The difference is, he's honest, and doesn't tolerate those who aren't. Dunnigan has the money to hire the best and in large numbers. He's not above using cattlemen's livestock-detectives and fast guns. Many are ex-rangers, some ex-marshals, and a few are ex-military. His resources far outweigh what small ranchers have available. And that's where we might have an edge on these rustlers. There's a possibility he'd be willing to help us out."

"How's that?" Jake was intrigued at the extent of Drew's knowledge.

"Dunnigan wants to expand his holdings to this region. That's one reason I'm here, to check out the market, see if it's an area where he could make a profitable investment. He might be willing to share resources if he believes it will benefit his growth plans." Drew was hesitant to share more. He knew a lot of ranchers didn't take kindly to Easterners moving in and buying up distressed ranches, even if they received a fair price. In Drew's opinion, it was a better option than simply walking away, but not many cattlemen agreed with him. "I'll telegraph him tomorrow. But tonight, gentlemen, I'm off to bed."

Will watched his brother walk up the steps and into the house. He appreciated Drew's ideas but didn't want him to stay, especially now, when there was more at stake than bringing Hollis to justice. Will knew Hollis was the man he'd tracked for five long years. He just needed time to prove it.

******

"I understand you're headed to town. I'd like to tag along, pick up some things." It had been a restless night for Tess. She hadn't been able to sleep and had opened her bedroom window for air. She had heard the voices and knelt below the opening to listen. What she had heard frightened her more than she'd let on to Amanda or Jake. She'd never learned to handle a gun as well as her friend, but she was determined to be of use if they found themselves in danger.

"Not planning to stay in town long, Tessa. What do you need? I'll be glad to pick up your supplies." Drew didn't want the woman near him. Something about her bothered him, but he couldn't pinpoint what.

"I don't need much time. There are only a few things and I'd really like to get away for a couple of hours, if it wouldn't be too much

119

trouble. We won't need the wagon. I'll just ride along with you."

"Morning, Drew, Tess. Is the coffee made?" Amanda entered the room rubbing her eyes and looking as if she hadn't slept at all.

"Why don't you sit, and I'll get some for you. Drew's going to town and I'm trying to convince him to let me tag along."

"Good idea. I need a few things, also," Amanda said.

Drew knew he'd lost the battle. There was no chance he'd make it off the ranch alone. "Get ready while I start saddling the horses." Drew rinsed his cup and headed outside.

"Doesn't sound too happy about you going with him, does he?" Amanda glanced at Tess.

"It doesn't matter if he's happy about it or not. He's staying here, as our guest, and I figure the least he can do is accompany me to town. Not sure how safe I feel riding alone with all that's going on. How about you, are you sure you're all right? Should I stay?"

"No, go. I'm doing fine. The sleep helped and I have a ton of chores. I figure Jake has some ideas about how he wants to handle what happened last night. Same with Will. Best if I talk to them now." Amanda pushed out of her chair and started outside.

"It wasn't your fault, you know." Tess had turned to look at her friend. She knew Amanda had lied about sleeping. She doubted if she'd slept at all.

Amanda kept her head down. She didn't respond for several moments. "The hard part isn't so much that I killed a man for trying to rustle our horses. Someone like that would've hung anyway. It's that I knew him, trusted him. I just wish I knew why," she said before grabbing a hat and walking out the back door.

******

They rode in silence for most of the trip, each lost in their own thoughts.

Drew's mind kept circling back to the shootings and the feeling that Mullins wasn't involved in the rustlings. Even though as an attorney he handled business issues, he still did his fair share of interviews, and sorted out the truth from lies more often than he liked. Nothing about Johnny being involved made sense, other than the fact he was with Alts. He wondered if the kid was simply in the wrong place at the wrong time. The thought brought to mind the anguished images of his brother, Will, after Emily's death. Inconsolable is how Aunt Alicia had described him. It wasn't his brother's fault, even though he blamed himself. Another case of wrong place, wrong time.

"You handle a gun well, at least that's what Amanda told me." Tess shot a look at Drew.

"Pardon me?" Drew shook himself out of his own mental ramblings.

"Well, Amanda said you're a good shot, like your brother. Neither of us was sure about

121

how you'd handle yourself when things got tough, but she says you do real well."

"That so? I suppose there's a compliment in there somewhere, if I thought hard enough about it anyway." Drew's comment and slight chuckle made Tess blush. She was actually kind of pretty, Drew thought, if one looked hard enough. "We grew up on the ranch, side by side. I learned all the same things he did, except I went off to college when I was nineteen. Of the four of us, he's the natural born rancher. Has the feel for it––cattle, horses, land. He should be there now, not chasing..." Drew stopped himself, irritated that he'd said that much.

"Not chasing what, Drew?" Tess asked when she realized he had no intention of finishing the thought.

"Nothing. He should just be back at our ranch, that's all."

"And you? Why aren't you there?"

"I will be soon enough, but I've got unfinished business in Denver before I can make a clean break with my boss. He's a good man. Tough, but fair, and I aim to leave on good terms."

They continued in silence for a few more minutes before Tess built up the courage to ask her question. "Would you teach me to shoot?"

The question surprised Drew. "Thought you'd already know how to handle a gun, with growing up on the ranch. You've never learned?"

122

"Oh, I know how to load and shoot, but I'm not good. Not like Amanda. I don't want to worry her, but I think there's more going on, more danger than we thought at first. If anyone comes to the ranch threatening us, I want to be prepared to do more than load a gun and fire. I want to feel I can hit what I'm aiming at."

"You want me to teach you to kill a man, is that it?"

"Well, I guess that's what I'm asking. Will you do it?"

Drew was silent so long that Tess thought he wouldn't answer.

"Don't know, Tessa. I'm not sure how long I'll be around Cold Creek. Isn't there someone else who could teach you? Jake maybe?"

The disappointment in Tessa's voice was evident, but she accepted his refusal to help her. "That's okay, I'll just ask Tinder. He's pretty good, a little impatient, but I'm sure he'd find the time." Tess had no plans to ask Tinder or Jake or any other ranch hand. She didn't want anyone there to know how incompetent she was with a gun. She'd just go out and learn on her own if Drew wouldn't help her.

"Makes sense. Appears he'll be at the ranch the rest of his life, so that gives him a lot of time to teach you." Drew knew it was the best solution, but darned if he didn't feel lousy about it.

It wasn't long before they entered the town of Cold Creek. Neither had spoken another word after Drew had rejected her request. She didn't seem angry, which surprised him. He was used to women using all kinds of tactics to get their way—pouting, sulking, yelling, threatening. It was one reason he'd never looked too seriously at marriage. Niall, Jamie, and Will had all fallen in love with wonderful women. Drew wondered if he'd ever be that fortunate. As much as the thought of a family and children felt right, the theatrics just never seemed worth it to him.

At just under a thousand people, Cold Creek wasn't small, but sure wasn't big by Drew's standards. Railroads didn't stop here, but the stage still came through on a regular basis, and by the size of the crowd, it appeared one had just arrived.

"Quite a commotion about a stage arrival, don't you think?" Drew asked as they rode closer to the stagecoach.

"It comes three to four times a week. Brings in people who get off the train in Great Valley." Tess looked toward the stage to focus on the passengers who were just climbing down. "Oh, Lord, it's Grant and Eleanor." She turned excitedly to Drew and urged her horse forward at a faster pace. "You know, Amanda and Joey's parents." Then she turned back to smile at Drew before continuing toward the stage. It was the first pure smile he'd seen from her. It lit up her face and hit him like a punch. She truly was pretty when she smiled.

"Grant! Eleanor!" Tess rode forward, then repeated the greeting, waving a hand at her long-time friends before getting off her horse.

"Grant, look. There's Tessa." Eleanor touched her husband's arm and pointed toward the young woman walking toward them. "But who's the man with her?"

"Don't know, but I aim to find out right now." Grant's smile was broad as he approached Tess and her companion. He pulled her into a brief hug before Eleanor came up and grabbed Tess's attention.

"It's so good you're home. We've all missed you, especially Amanda and Joey. But why didn't you send word about getting in today? They'd have come to meet you."

"We wanted to surprise everyone. Didn't expect to run into you in town. And, who's your friend?" Grant took in the tall, well-built man standing next to Tess.

"This is Drew MacLaren. He's staying at the ranch for a spell. His brother, Will, is working for us."

"Mr. Taylor, Mrs. Taylor," Drew shook Grant's hand and nodded to Eleanor, "it's a pleasure to meet you. I hope I'm not intruding, staying at the ranch, I mean."

"If Amanda or Tess invited you, then you're welcome to visit." Grant emphasized the last word just enough so Drew would get the meaning.

"I won't be here long, Mr. Taylor. Just came to help my brother with some, uh, family business, then I'll be returning to Denver."

"You're from Denver, then?" Eleanor asked, wanting to know more about the man who'd accompanied Tess to town. It was unusual for Tess to leave the ranch with anyone she hadn't known for some time.

"No, ma'am, I'm from Arizona, but my job is in Denver. I plan to return to Arizona at some point soon, though."

"Well, Eleanor, I say we get a wagon and start for home." Grant turned to a man about ten feet away. "Jack? You mind finding us transportation to the ranch and getting someone to load the luggage?"

"No, Sir, Mr. Taylor. I'll get to it right now." The man was already on his way as the last words left his mouth.

"Drew has a couple of things to do and I have to pick up some supplies, but we'd like to ride back with you, right, Drew?" Tess looked over and up at her companion. For some reason it had never registered with her that he was such a tall man. She estimated six-feet plus a few inches. At five-eight she considered herself a tall woman, but he towered over her.

"Of course, Tess. I'll meet you in front of the general store as soon as I'm through." Drew nodded at the Taylor's and Tess before walking down the street toward the telegraph office. He'd send the request off to his boss, Louis Dunnigan, and then send another message to Fire Mountain. He needed to let Niall and Jamie know what was happening.

Chapter Fourteen

"All four dead? Tell me what happened, Hollis, and I want it straight." The boss stood at the top of a ridge, looking down on his ranch. A good spread, but too much rock, not enough pasture. That would change soon.

"Jake and MacLaren must've figured something was going on and followed us. We got trapped in the canyon with the horses and had no choice but to run. I'm the only one who made it."

"Even Alts?" The boss's face was grim but he showed no other emotions.

"Yea, Alts, too." Hollis didn't tell the man that Alts had died by his gun and not at the canyon. No reason the boss had to know. Hollis went on to explain how Johnny Mullins had been in the area, unaware of the danger or his imminent death.

"Johnny's death is a problem. Grant liked the boy—thought he might take over from Jake someday." The boss turned back to the canyon and thought of his young wife. He wondered if he'd have handled things in a different way if she'd come into his life sooner.

Vengeance and greed had molded him into a man who'd do anything to get even with the one person he had thought would always stand by him, his best friend. But the man had betrayed him, pushed him out just as success

127

was within their grasp. Over the years he'd done what little he could to settle the score—freak accidents, poisoned waterholes, missing cattle—but it had never been enough for him. He'd wanted to hurt Taylor, run him into the ground, make him give up.

In time he came to realize his actions were too small, insignificant to a man like Grant, and he'd hired Hollis to put a real dent in the Big G by stealing cattle and Taylor's prized horse stock. Chet had been very willing to hire the men needed to rustle, not only from Taylor, but from other neighboring ranches. Hollis had his own plans, driven by greed and his desire for Grant's daughter. Now their plans were jeopardized by the deaths of four men. They'd need to make changes. He had to work with reality, and that meant closing the operation, soon. "Meet me here again at midnight. And Chet, don't do anything more until then."

******

Amanda walked into the barn after finishing her chores and spotted Will sitting on a small bench. "Do you know where I can find Jake?"

"He rode out with a few men to check fences on the south border. Took Tinder with him." Will didn't turn from the repair work that held his attention.

"I want to know what's next. What do we need to do to protect the cattle, the horses?"

"Best for you to talk with Jake. He's your foreman—it should come from him."

"Well, he's not here and I'm asking you." Amanda walked up to within a few feet of Will, hands on hips, eyes not wavering from his. "I won't be cut out of this."

He continued to sit but stared right back at her. "Look, I don't know for certain what Jake plans, or how I fit into it, other than continue to ride fence lines." Will looked back at the leather in his hands and tried to ignore the woman who still stood next to him. He could feel the heat pouring from her. Whether it was from anger or something else, he didn't know.

"Don't dismiss me, Will. The three of you must have shared your thoughts after I went upstairs last night. I need answers, need to know what to expect, and how to stop the rustling. Jake's not here, but you are, and I suspect you know what he plans. Please, tell me." She placed a hand on Will's arm.

He put the piece of leather on a small table and pushed his tall frame from the bench. Her hand fell away. He missed the warmth of her touch immediately and stepped back to gain some distance. Being this close to Amanda, without others around, wasn't a smart idea. There was too much pull between them. All he could think about when she was around was their kiss and how he had wanted it to continue, and how much he wanted to pull her to him now.

"All I know for sure is that he plans to bring the cattle as close-in as possible—into one large herd—and post extra men. He wants to keep watch twenty-four hours a day. Most likely he, Drew, and I will rotate shifts so that one of us is always with the herd. Drew rode to town to send a telegram to his boss in Denver. He thinks Dunnigan may agree to help with some extra men——men trained to look for rustlers and deal with them. No guarantees, but Drew believes it's worth a try." Will plunged his hands into his pockets and turned to leave.

"That's all? What about warning the other ranchers, hiring more men, and contacting the Colorado Rangers?" Amanda followed him toward the barn entrance.

"Jake sent a man out to let the neighboring ranchers know what happened. Drew's boss has contacts with the Rangers. He's hoping we'll get some support from them."

Amanda stopped at one of the stalls. She placed a hand on the nearest post to peer over at the six-month-old colt inside. If all went well, they hoped he would be the foundation of a new breeding program that Tessa had talked Grant into starting. But it would all be put at risk if they didn't stop the rustlers. Taking cattle was one thing, but stealing horses made it much more serious in the eyes of the ranchers.

"Amanda, are you all right?" She was so lost in her thoughts she hadn't noticed Will come back to stand beside her. Although he kept his hands stashed in his pockets, he stood only a foot away and the closeness unsettled her.

"I'm fine, just worried about all that's happened. Jake's a wonderful foreman, but older, and I know Drew plans to leave for Denver soon. It's become clear to me you're here for other reasons than a ranch job. We both know you're much more than a basic hand. This is a short-term job for you, isn't it Will?"

Will looked uncomfortable as he gazed down into her troubled eyes. He could lie, but that would serve no purpose. She'd guessed right. He planned to finish his business with Hollis then head home, to Fire Mountain. But standing here, inches away, made his determination to distance himself from Amanda harder than he'd thought. What he saw in her eyes mirrored his own—desire and a longing to continue what they'd started only days before. He pulled a hand from a pocket and lifted it to gently brush strands of hair off her face and hook it behind an ear before letting his fingers gently caress her cheek, before cupping it with his palm. She leaned into him and brought one hand up to cover his. He placed his other hand on her shoulder and turned her to him.

"Amanda, how I wish things could be different. But I'm not the man you believe me to be." His words were soft but there was no mistaking the yearning in his voice.

Amanda raised her eyes to study his face, looking for confirmation of his words, but she found none. "No, Will, you are exactly the man I believe you to be. I wouldn't want you to be anyone else." She lifted a hand to his shoulder and leaned up to place a kiss on his unshaven cheek.

At Amanda's touch, Will turned to her and drew her close. His lips brushed across hers so lightly she had little time to acknowledge the contact. Then his mouth settled more firmly on hers and she responded fully, wrapping her arms around his neck to pull him towards her. He sipped at her lips until she opened and his tongue began a dance with hers. He kept one hand on her back while the other moved to a hip, then up to caress her stomach before continuing the upward journey to cup a breast. A sigh escaped her as his hand moved over her in a gentle caress, causing heat to flare between them.

Neither noticed that their bodies were flush and she was now backed up to the stall railing, her legs between his. His lips left hers to move down her neck to the top of her blouse. Her head fell back and he placed soft kisses along the small exposed opening before traveling back up to capture her mouth again.

The sound of wagon wheels and a shout of, "Whoa," pierced the quiet of the barn. Will dropped his arms and stepped back as both tried to calm their breathing and adjust to the sudden lack of contact.

"I'll get Amanda, Grant. She's probably in the house." Amanda and Will recognized Tess's voice.

"Pa! Ma! You're back." It was Joey this time.

Amanda looked up at Will before starting for the door. "It's my parents." Her words were rough, quiet. *What was I thinking? And after all my internal promises to stay away from this man.* "Come on, I'll introduce you." She stepped further ahead of Will as they approached the barn entrance. "I'm here, Tess," she called out, then ran to hug her mother, who stood next to the wagon.

Eleanor returned her daughter's embrace while staring at the man behind her. Her head shifted to Drew, then back again at the stranger. Other than the clothes, the two men were identical. "So, you must be Drew's brother." She walked up to Will. Amanda took the opportunity to run into her father's outstretched arms.

Will pulled off his hat. "Yes, ma'am. I'm Will MacLaren. I take it you've met my brother."

"Yes, we happened upon them in town." Eleanor continued to stare at the two men as Drew walked up beside them.

"So, this is the brother," a voice boomed from behind Amanda's mother. "Grant Taylor." He reached out a hand to grasp the one Will offered.

"Will MacLaren, Mr. Taylor."

"Call me Grant, or boss, but not Mr. Taylor. Makes me feel old. Glad to hear you've been helping Jake and Amanda. Also heard we've got trouble. As soon as I get Eleanor settled, let's meet in my office so you can fill me in." Grant looked between Will and Drew.

"Yes, sir," they both answered, then walked back to the wagon to help unload the luggage and carry it into the house.

Tess watched in silence from the porch as the scene played out. At one time she would have had a father, a mother, to welcome home, but not now. The ache hit hard, but passed within moments. She was used to the dull ache of having no family, but for some reason it never got any easier.

******

The pain was intense. He lay on his back and stared up at dusty, spider-infested rafters. Sunlight streamed through cracks in the old roof and he could hear the constant buzz of insects. He tried to sit up, but his left shoulder wouldn't cooperate. Rolling to his side he used his right arm for leverage to push to his knees. The pain was sharp and surged from his shoulder down the length of his arm. Blood soaked through his jacket. He took a deep breath and willed his body to stand. He looked around the small cabin, and remembered. Hollis. The man had shot him.

Frank Alts pulled back his jacket, then his vest, to reveal the shirt below. Something pinched his skin. He'd moved his badge from his pocket to his shirt just before the meeting with Hollis, but right now, he couldn't remember why. It was now bent and poking into his skin. A searing pain came from a hole in his left shoulder. Reality hit quick. Changing the badge's location had saved his life. Hollis' bullet must have hit his badge, deflecting it just enough to miss his heart and pierce his left shoulder. Hurt like hell, but he was alive.

Sweat poured off Frank as he looked around for something to clean the wound. Nothing. He held his injured shoulder tight to his side and limped out the door. He'd have to hike down the long trail to find help. His horse and guns were gone but at least he could walk. He took one last look at the cabin, then began the journey down the mountain.

******

"I told you we had to get it done before Taylor got home. Now there's no choice but to close up and clear out with the cattle while there's still a chance to make some money." Sheriff Dutton paced the small office and peered out the window to make sure no one was outside. "Tonight, Chet. No more stalling."

"Taylor doesn't have any idea it's us, and he won't find out. I told you, Alts is dead and the others won't say a word. The real money is in the horses, and I aim to grab them before

135

we clear out." Hollis pulled a thin cheroot from his jacket and lit up. He sat back in the chair, relaxed, giving the impression of calm when he was just as concerned as Dutton. He'd give up on his dream of the girl, but he wouldn't give up on taking the horses from the Taylor ranch. They were some of the best mounts in the state and would bring good money in Wyoming or Montana.

"No, Chet. We have to leave now, tonight, with the cattle. Forget the horses. It's not worth the risk now that they've been moved to the ranch." Dutton just didn't understand the man's reluctance to get out while they still could. The cattle would bring enough money to start over somewhere else––out of the reach of Will MacLaren.

Hollis crushed the cheroot on the floor and stood. He was a good five inches taller than Dutton, but fifty pounds lighter. He'd like to take care of the man now but it would have to wait until they were away from town. The sheriff had become a liability. He'd need to be taken care of the same as Alts.

"Tell you what, we'll ride out to the see the boys and tell them to be ready to move in two days. You can stay with them. Take what you need and let the deputy know you'll be gone a couple days. We'll be out of the area by the time he realizes you aren't coming back."

"Good, Chet, that's good. I'll meet you outside of town in an hour." Dutton was surprised at Chet's decision, but relieved. It was time they moved on to where no one recognized Hollis. Dutton would take his cut and get as far away from the man as possible.

Chapter Fifteen

"Alts, huh? Never met the man. Jake must've hired him after I left." Grant sat at his desk and listened as Will explained the activities of the last few weeks.

"There's something else you should know." Will dreaded what he had to say but knew it had to be done. "Johnny Mullins was riding with Alts. He was shot and killed when we caught them in the canyon." Will paused for a moment before he continued. "Amanda fired the shot that killed him."

Grant's face contorted. He sprang from his chair and slammed his fist onto the desk. "Who allowed my daughter to go out on a night raid, after rustlers?" he bellowed. "She could've been killed."

The office door burst open. Amanda and Eleanor stormed into the room, but stopped when they saw that all seemed fine. Amanda's father was known for his calm disposition and slow temper. The outburst they'd heard had surprised both women.

"Grant, what is going on in here? We could hear you in the kitchen." Eleanor walked up to her husband and looked around, as if trying to find the source of his outburst.

"It's my fault, ma'am. I just gave your husband some news he didn't want to hear." Will shot a meaningful glance at Amanda. He saw her eyes widen as she grasped his meaning.

"Do you want to tell me what possessed you to go out at night, with the men, after a group of rustlers? What the hell were you thinking?" Grant seldom swore in front of the women, and worked hard to control his anger, but the thought that he could've lost Amanda, never seen her again, shot tremors through his normally stoic frame.

"Father, I can explain..."

"Oh, can you now? And can you explain shooting a man?"

"Shooting a man? What do you mean, Grant?" Eleanor's composure began to crack at the knowledge that her daughter may have hurt someone.

"Yes, Eleanor. Shot and killed a man. Johnny Mullins," Grant said.

"Johnny? He's dead?" Eleanor face drained of color. She looked at her daughter before lowering herself into a nearby chair.

"Father, if you'd just let me explain," Amanda tried again. When her father didn't respond, she continued. "I made them take me. None of them—Jake, Will, or Drew—wanted me to go, but I forced it."

"We should've tried harder to stop her, sir." Drew said. "I've never seen someone so determined not to be left behind."

"They couldn't have stopped me, Father. I would have followed them. It's no one's fault but mine that I was out there." She walked up to her father and fixed her eyes on him. "And I'd do it again."

Her father said nothing, just continued to stare at his daughter and come to terms with the fact that she'd done something he'd prayed she'd never do.

"But why would you shoot Johnny?" her mother asked.

"He was with them, Mother. He rode out with Frank Alts and was in the canyon where we keep the remuda. Two other men were with them. When Will called out to let them know we were there, they started to shoot. Alts and Johnny were able to get past Jake, Will, and Drew. I was the last person with any chance to stop them. I didn't know it was Johnny until it was too late."

"He was alive when we got to him, but he didn't offer an explanation. Just said he shouldn't have gone with them." Will walked over to stand by Amanda just as the office door opened.

Tess stepped inside and looked around at the people in the room. "Is everything all right, Amanda?"

"Yes, everything is fine. We were explaining about Johnny to Mother and Father."

"Did you go with them too, Tess?" Grant asked.

"No. I didn't know they'd left until I went looking for Amanda and found her horse was gone. It was when they returned that I learned what had happened."

140

The room was silent for a moment before Will broke the silence. "Drew and I have a few things to take care of——if we're through here."

"Yes, we're through, for now," Grant said.

Amanda and Tess began to leave with the men before Grant stopped them. "I'd like you two to stay. Eleanor and I have some things to explain, and this appears to be a good time."

The two young women glanced at each other but did as Grant asked.

"Sit down, girls. This may take some time," Eleanor said when the two continued to stand in front of the desk.

"This all sounds quite mysterious, Mother."

"In some ways it may seem so, dear. Your Father and I had much time to talk on our travels, sort some things out that had been haunting us for a long time. We made the decision that it was time we told you girls more details about the past. You're both old enough and there's no point in waiting any longer."

Grant walked over to the chair where Eleanor sat and placed a hand on his wife's shoulder. They smiled at each other before Eleanor nodded for him to continue.

"Amanda, how much do you remember about your Mother leaving for Europe when you were about a year old?"

Amanda's eyes swept to her mother's. "I was just a baby. I never knew she left. How long were you gone, Mother?"

"Almost a year. It was a hard time for your father and me. I met your father when he came to London for business and we fell in love. My parents objected, of course. He was a rough American, and a rancher. The combination was quite beyond them. But after a while they accepted my desire to marry Grant. I was young, and never quite acclimated to ranch life. I'd grown up with servants, balls, grand holidays, and all the wonderful things my parents provided. I had help here, of course, but the work was unending and the social connections non-existent." Eleanor looked up at Tessa. "Your mother—Julia—was my only friend. I was very lonely. Grant and I had spoken of me returning to England for a long visit, but then I became pregnant with you, Amanda, and leaving seemed impossible."

Grant leaned down to whisper in his wife's ear. When she nodded, he continued. "She was miserable, Amanda. She loved you, but she needed to leave, decide if she wanted to continue her life with me in Colorado or stay permanently in England. It was hard on both of us. You were so small, but we had help at that time and I encouraged her to go. I wanted it to be decided one way or another before you were old enough to remember her absence." Grant walked over to a table, grabbed a bottle and poured a drink. He downed it in one swallow before turning back to the women. He took a deep breath and continued.

"Her absence was painful and I was incredibly lonely without her." He poured another drink and shot it down his throat, letting the amber liquid work its magic. Amanda had never seen her Father drink during the day. She knew there was more to come but had no idea what could upset her parents so much.

"Tess, your Mother and Father lived at the ranch at that time. Bobby had worked for me about two years when Eleanor left for England. He knew it was hard for me to be away from the ranch for long periods, so he volunteered to do most of the traveling." He glanced once more at his wife before going on. "There's no easy way to say this, but Julia and I had always been drawn to each other. Knowing this, and that my marriage with Eleanor was strained, Julia made it a point to never be around me without Bobby. Neither of us had any intention of ever acting on our feelings."

"No." The word escaped Tess's lips before she could stop it. She started to rise, but Amanda's hand grasped her arm, encouraging her to stay and hear Grant out.

"It wasn't her fault, Tess, it was mine. Bobby was gone, Amanda was having a bad night, and I walked over to your parents' cabin to get help from Julia. She always had an amazing way with Amanda. Within minutes she had her calmed down and asleep, but we were both exhausted. She offered to make coffee. I wish I could tell you how it happened, but all I can say is that it simply did. It was just the one time and each of us felt terrible about the betrayal. Within a few weeks, Julia realized she was pregnant, with you, Tess." Grant paused to see if Tess comprehended his meaning.

Tess jumped from her chair and stormed toward Grant. "How can you say these things about my mother? She was a good person. She loved my father. Why would you do this?" Tears began to roll down her cheeks but she swiped them away.

"We're telling you now because you have a right to know that you're my daughter, and Amanda's half-sister." Grant looked at his empty glass and wished he could down the entire bottle.

"But how do you know I'm your daughter? How could you know?" Tess's voice was strained and laced with disbelief.

"Bobby and Julia had tried for years to have children. They'd given up. Julia knew immediately that the child was mine, and it was confirmed after you were born. You were the exact image of my mother. Eleanor had returned from England by then, determined to build a life with Amanda and me. But it only took Eleanor one look at you, Tess, and she knew you were mine and not Robert's."

Tess stared at Eleanor, then at Grant. It was too much. "No! This can't be true. Father would have told me."

"He never knew." Eleanor walked up to the young woman she loved as much as her own daughter. She tried to place an arm around Tess's shoulders but Tess shook her off. "We all thought it better he not know. Robert was so thrilled with being a father, and he loved you so much, that we decided there was no point in ever telling him. Maybe it was wrong, but Julia was firm that he not know."

"But you, Eleanor?" Tess asked. "Why did you stay with Grant after you knew?"

"Because I love him, Tess. It took my going to England to realize just how much. And, when I returned, I had to face the fact that much of it was my fault. I truly believe it would not have happened if I had stayed by his side and not left for my own selfish reasons." She walked to Grant and grabbed his hand.

Grant knew that Eleanor had been devastated by his betrayal. Looking back, neither understood why she hadn't left and taken Amanda with her. But she'd stayed, and over time, had worked through the pain and bitterness. Eleanor had even continued her friendship with Julia, although only God knew how. Grant still thanked God each day that his wife had stuck by him and accepted Tess as his daughter.

The room fell silent. Tess sat back in her chair, placed her hands in her lap, but couldn't control the shaking. Grant walked over to stand in front of her, but she stood and ran from the room before anyone could stop her.

"Let her go, Grant. She needs time to think through all she's learned. It will work out, in time." Eleanor's soothing words stopped her husband when he made a move to go after Tess.

Amanda sat in silence on the other side of the room. She couldn't get past the realization that Tess was her half-sister or that her father had betrayed her mother. She found it hard to look at either of her parents. All these years they'd held the secret.

"Amanda?" Her Mother's voice pierced through her clouded mind. She looked up to a face filled with love. "We never meant to hurt either of you. But it was time you both learned the truth."

"I'll go, Mother." Amanda stood to walk towards the door. She needed to get out of the house, away from her parents. She wanted time to sort through all she'd learned.

"Go where, Amanda?" Grant interjected. He hoped his wife was right, that both of his daughters would accept the truth.

"To find Tess. She might talk with me."

Amanda walked out of the office, certain she knew the exact place where Tess would go.

Chapter Sixteen

"My horse is acting up," Hollis lied. "I need to check to see if he picked up a stone." They were several miles from town, up an old deer trail, on their way to the camp where Chet's men kept the stolen cattle. The growth was dense in the area. It'd be a hard place to find a man, or a body.

Dutton dismounted. "Fine with me. I need to take care of business anyway." The sheriff made his way behind a brush, unaware that Hollis was only a few feet behind. Before the man knew what Chet had planned, he heard a shot, felt pain to his back, and slumped to the ground. Dutton was dead.

"That, Sheriff, is what happens to men with no guts and no vision," Hollis spit on the ground beside the body. He holstered his gun and reached down to drag the body further into the brush. Chet wanted it as far away from the trail as possible even though he doubted anyone would ever come across it. He found a natural ditch a hundred feet away and dumped the sheriff in. Before he left, he took Dutton's gun, covered him with loose dirt, and pulled fallen brush over him. No, he didn't think anyone would ever find this body.

******

"Tess, you in there?" Amanda made her way up the path towards a cave that was a secret only the two of them shared. At least they thought of it that way. "Tess, it's Amanda. I just want to talk for a bit."

She tried again when there was no response. "Tess, I know you're in here."

"I'm not in the mood to talk, Amanda. Just let me be alone a while."

At least Amanda knew Tess was in the cave. She had no intention of returning to the house without her friend––her half-sister. The thought made her smile even as she was still trying to adjust to the circumstances, and the knowledge that her father was also Tess's.

Amanda entered the cave and spotted Tess about ten feet inside, sitting cross-legged on the ground. She picked her way over the rocky floor and lowered herself next to her. They sat in silence for several minutes, each lost in her own thoughts.

"Why now? They could have said something years ago, after my father died."

"I've been wondering the same thing and don't know for sure, but seems to me they felt we weren't ready to learn the truth until now. Maybe they thought we couldn't handle it." Amanda considered something else. "Did you hear Mother say that she and Father had talked about this on their trip? I wonder if they had never truly come to terms with it between themselves. I love Father, but the way he hurt my mother is something I can't understand. Nor how Mother forgave him and

148

continued to live at the ranch. I don't know that I could do it." Her voice trailed off. She began to pick at the loose rocks at her feet, finally throwing the largest one against a wall of the cave.

"I loved my parents. I can't seem to think of them as anything else."

"Well, you don't have to. Julia will always be your mother, and Bobby, as far as your heart knows, your father. Nothing can ever change that. But, I think it's good to know about Grant. He's always loved you, and now I understand why."

Tess picked up a stone and rolled it around in her palm, feeling the weight as well as the texture. A deep sigh escaped her just before she threw it against the wall. It landed right next to Amanda's. "Well, like Eleanor said, she's always loved Grant. She has a big heart. I know my Mother loved her and thought of Eleanor as her closest friend." Tears began to pool in the young woman's eyes as she drew her knees up, placed her arms across them, and rested her head.

"It's not so bad, is it? Having me for a sister?" Amanda glanced over at Tess and smiled.

Tess lifted her head. "I guess that's the only good part of this. I've always felt real close to you, closer than friends. Now I know why."

Amanda reached over, took one of Tess's hands in hers, and squeezed. "I'd say that's the best news I've heard in a very long time."

******

"Can I help you?" the deputy looked up to see a stranger enter the jail.

"Possibly. Looking for the Taylor place. Can you tell me how to get there?"

"Sure can. Go north out of town and follow the road a few miles to a split. Go right, away from the mountains, towards the low hills. You can't miss it. It's the only spread up that direction."

"Thanks."

"Hey, I didn't get your name," the deputy called to the departing figure.

"MacLaren. Jamie MacLaren."

Jamie continued walking down the wooden boardwalk to one of two saloons on the main street. Unlike Fire Mountain, which was large enough to support a dozen drinking establishments, Cold Creek appeared lucky to support two. It had been a long trip and he planned to grab a whiskey, or two, before he continued.

"What are you having, mister?"

"Whiskey."

"You're not from around here, are you?" The bartender placed a shot glass in front of Jamie.

"No, just visiting."

"That right? And who might that be?"

Jamie just looked over the shot glass at the man, downed his drink, threw some coin on the bar, and walked off. He didn't share information much, and certainly not without knowing more about the dangers this town held for his brother.

A young man slammed into Jamie on the walkway outside the saloon. "Sorry, mister. My fault. Hope you're okay."

Jamie couldn't help but chuckle at the comment. He was over six feet tall and the young man who'd bumped into him was no more than five-feet-eight.

"Do I know you, mister? You look real familiar."

"Doubt it. I just got into town."

The young man stuck out his hand before Jamie could walk away. "Tinder's what they call me."

"Tinder, huh? Jamie MacLaren." Jamie took the offered hand.

"MacLaren. That's why you look familiar. Two MacLarens are staying out at the ranch. They your kin?"

"Brothers. I'm headed out to see them."

"Well, you just hold on a few minutes and I'll ride out with you. Not hard to find, but better with someone who knows the way."

An hour later the two men dismounted in front of a large house and tied their horses to the post out front. Tinder bounded up the steps, knocked a couple of times, then opened the door. "Boss, someone here to see you," he called inside.

"What is it, Tinder?" Grant walked out of his office.

"Another MacLaren showed up in town. Thought it best to bring him out here myself."

Grant moved past his ranch hand, toward the stranger standing on the porch.

"Mr. Taylor?"

"That's me. You another one of those MacLaren brothers?"

"Yes, sir. Jamie MacLaren. Hope my younger brothers haven't caused you any trouble." Jamie looked past the man into the large living area of the house. The MacLaren main house was large, but judging by what he could see, this place was at least twice the size.

"No trouble at all. Glad to have them. We've been experiencing some cattle rustling and your brothers have been helping us out. Come on in. I'll get you a drink and we can talk until they get back."

"Back?"

"Yea. Got them riding fence on the north end. That's where most of the cattle have gone missing."

Jamie let out a chest-rumbling laugh at that news. "Riding fence? Drew and Will? Well, that I'd like to see. Glad to see someone is putting all the skills they packed away years ago to use." He smiled at his host. "I'd love that drink, Mr. Taylor."

"Grant. Call me Grant."

******

"What do you think, Drew?" Will asked as they made their way back to the ranch. They'd ridden out right after informing Grant of the missing cattle and Johnny's death.

"Well, it seems pretty obvious they're taking the cattle through the north boundary, then heading west. I'm thinking we should take a group of men that way tomorrow and see if we can find where they're holding them. The more men the better."

"It seems too easy, but you can't argue with all the tracks." Will looked at the house before turning his horse toward the barn. He wanted to see Amanda. They had barely spoken since their encounter that morning. "Wish we had more men. We could use at least half a dozen more. No telling how many men are guarding the cattle, but there must be a lot based on the number of animals that are missing."

"You ever think there might be a connection between the rustling and Hollis?" Drew asked.

"Well, the thought has crossed my mind. Truth is, with so much happening, I haven't had much time to think about Hollis the past week. But that's going to change. I need to confront the man and bring this to an end."

"Legally, right, Will?"

"Hell, you must know by now I don't care how it happens. All I know is the man is going to pay for what he did to Emily." Will's jaw was set and Drew knew it would do no good to discuss it further this evening.

The two unsaddled their horses and turned them out into the small pasture next to the barn. The sound of laughter had both turning their heads to see Amanda and Tess approaching. One look at Amanda and Will's stomach dropped. *Damn but she's pretty.* He realized as soon as the thought was out that it had no place in his head. Catching Hollis was the only reason he was in Cold Creek. He'd take care of the man who murdered his wife, track down the cattle, and ride home to Fire Mountain.

"Where have you two been?" Drew stared at both women but focused his attention on Tess. *She certainly is a very attractive woman.* There was a softness, a kindness about her that touched him. Plus, she had a deep concern about the Taylors and the ranch. Someday he'd like to find someone like her, move back home, and work with Will to breed the finest horse stock in Arizona, possibly the West. As much as he'd like to explore his feelings for Tess, he knew it wasn't wise. His life was in Denver, and after that, in Fire Mountain, not in a small town at the western edge of Colorado.

"Just back from a walk. You two ready to head in? Maria should have supper ready about now." Amanda smiled, but her questioning eyes locked onto Will's. She wondered if they'd have a chance to talk about what had happened in the barn that morning, and if it had the same impact on him that it had on her. Amanda knew she was losing her heart to this man and realized that it would only cause her pain when he rode out, leaving her behind.

The four heard male voices as they entered the house. Amanda and Tess had preceded them and walked toward the office. What the girls saw took their breath away. A very handsome man with dark auburn hair, whom neither had met before, sat talking with Grant.

"Oh my," Amanda said at the same time Tess's eyes went wide and a hand flew to her heart.

Will and Drew stopped in their tracks at the sight of Jamie, sitting in a large leather chair, smoking a cigar, and sipping whiskey. They each looked at their older brother, then back at the women.

"He's married," Will informed them in a brusque voice.

"Yea, with one son and another on the way," Drew added.

"And how would you know that?" Amanda asked.

"Because he's our brother, Jamie," Drew said.

At the mention of his name, Jamie looked around to see the twins enter the office with two very lovely ladies.

"Well, wondered when you'd decide to join us," Grant said. "Will and Drew, I believe you already know this gentleman."

"Yes, sir, we sure do." Drew clapped his older brother on the shoulder. "Good to see you, Jamie."

"Same here, Drew." Then he looked at Will. "Been a long time, Will. How are you?" Jamie asked as he took his brother's hand.

"I've been better. Wish I could say I'm happy to see you, but I'm sure you know I'm not."

"What you want right now means nothing to me, and you darn well know it. I'm here and I'm staying until this thing has played out." Jamie's voice was friendly but hard. Will knew he wouldn't budge.

Grant cleared his throat at the interesting exchange between the brothers. "Jamie, these are my daughters, Amanda and Tess."

"Daughters?" Drew and Will asked at the same time.

"Nice to meet you, ladies," Jamie said while casting a curious eye at the twins.

"There's a lot you missed after you left the meeting earlier. But, yes, Amanda and Tess are both my daughters. Now, shall we get some supper before Maria throws it out?"

Amanda took one of Jamie's arms while Tess took the other to accompany him to the supper table. "So, your brothers tell us you're married, Mr. MacLaren, and that you have children. Is that correct?" Amanda asked.

"It's Jamie, and yes, ma'am, I have one boy and a baby on the way."

Amanda smiled over her shoulder at Will who followed a few feet behind with an unmistakable scowl on his handsome face. She found herself wondering what the fourth brother looked like, and at that moment made a promise to herself that someday she'd find out.

Chapter Seventeen

"One last job, men, that's all we'll need to finish up in Cold Creek and move out." Hollis finished describing the plan to steal the Taylor horses the following night. The boss and Chet had met the night before and laid out the plans for closing up and moving the livestock. They'd use the horses as their remuda for driving the cattle to the train in Slider Junction, three days journey west of Cold Creek. It was a longer drive, but safer than going north to the closest station in Great Valley.

"What about the sheriff, Chet? Where do we meet up with him?" Del Wiley worked with Chet at the Bierdan ranch and was the first person the outlaw had brought into the group.

"He'll catch up when he can, Del. Any other questions?"

"Which group you riding with?" an older man asked.

"I'll be with those going to the Taylor ranch. Del will go with the other group. Anything else?" When no one else responded, Chet made his last comment. "This is it boys, what we've all worked for. If anyone interferes, kill them. Got that?"

Most nodded, but some looked at each other as if wondering what Hollis wasn't telling them. Each man had been hand-picked, and each knew the ruthlessness of their leader. No one wanted to cross him, and no one trusted him.

"We'll meet at the designated place tomorrow at midnight." Chet walked off, mounted, and turned his horse toward the Taylor ranch.

With Alts out of the way, Hollis had to take on the job of checking the Taylor layout before their raid. He didn't make mistakes often, but getting rid of Alts probably hadn't been his best move. Now he'd be the one sticking his neck out instead of some low-level rustler. Well, it was done, and there was no one left to handle it but him.

Hollis approached the ranch at a slow pace, watching to be sure there weren't men posted around the perimeter. He took a slow swing around and saw no one. Taylor had built a series of corrals, each bordering another, in a long row behind the barn. The horses Hollis wanted were in the largest corral near the back. It was the farthest location from both the main house and bunkhouse. Easy pickings, if his men could get to the gate undetected.

He left his horse behind and worked his way closer to the house. He'd heard Jake put out word that the ranch was looking for more men. That was only two days ago. Hollis heard laughter from the house and crept up just below a window to peer inside. He knew Grant was back, but sitting next to him at the table was a man he didn't recognize. Maybe Jake had found other men as well. Will and Drew MacLaren were at the table, also.

"Pass those potatoes this way, Jamie, unless you plan to finish them yourself," Drew said.

"Here you go, little brother. Wouldn't want to stop your growth spurt," Jamie replied as he passed the dish over and laughed.

Brother, thought Hollis. *Hell, another MacLaren*. He wondered if this one was as good with a gun as the other two. Didn't matter. He needed to focus on Grant being back. The man was a force in this area—someone you didn't mess with—which meant it was also easy for him to attract new ranch hands with short notice. Grant could bring them on fast, but not fast enough to stop a raid tomorrow night, Hollis decided. He'd stick with the plan as well as his decision to take what else he wanted.

******

Frank had finally made it down the hill to a slow running creek at the far edge of the Taylor ranch. The bleeding had stopped, but a throbbing pain indicated the wound might be infected. He cleaned it as best as possible in the stream, and sat back to rest, and think.

He should've hauled Chet in sooner, but he had wanted to give the other rangers time to get in place. Doing that had cost young Mullins his life. If only Frank had been able to tell Johnny what was happening, but at the time, he wasn't sure the young man wasn't involved with Hollis. Now Alts knew Johnny had only been an innocent in the wrong place. It was in the past. Frank needed to focus on stopping Hollis and getting home to his son, Aaron. This might very well be his last assignment as a Colorado Ranger. The excitement of his job had worn off long ago, and since his wife had up and left, there was no one but a widow woman to take care of Aaron when Frank was gone. He'd finish this last job, return to Denver, and become the father Aaron deserved.

******

"Tell me everything you know," Jamie commanded his brothers early the next morning. It had been late when they headed to bed the night before, each man exhausted from the long day.

"Like Grant already told you, one of the ranch hands has been in on the whole thing. Must've helped with the early rustling here, at Bierdan's ranch, and possibly at other spreads. He and Mullins were in the canyon with two others the night we found them. Three were killed, but the fourth man got away. Haven't seen him since." Will looked disgusted at their inability to identify where the fourth man had gone. He'd just disappeared.

"He work here long?" Jamie asked.

161

"A few months, but long enough to learn how Jake ran the place, and where the cattle and horses were kept," Drew said.

"Either of you get to know him?"

"Not really. Didn't get close. He stayed with Tinder and Mullins some of the time. Alts was a loner from what I could tell." Will hadn't gotten close to anyone during his brief time at the ranch. Hadn't planned to.

"Alts? The man's name is Alts?" The surprise on Jamie's face wasn't lost on his brothers.

"Yea, Frank Alts. You know him?" Drew asked.

"Ah, hell. I didn't know he was working this far from Denver." Jamie took off his hat, ran his hand through his hair, and paced a few feet before turning back to stand by his brothers. "Worked with him as a Marshal. Good man. He hired on with the Colorado Rangers when his wife up and left him with a young son. Moved to Denver. Mainly works cattle issues and rancher disputes. Surprised you never heard of him, Drew."

The news that their brother knew the man they'd thought of as a rustler surprised them.

"Never worked with him or heard of the man. Of course, I didn't work cattle disputes as much as land and purchase issues. Mr. Dunnigan is close with the head of the rangers in Denver. I can send another message to him today, find out if he can get us information on Alts," Drew replied.

"Well, he wasn't shot, didn't come back here, and hasn't turned up in town. He could be hiding out with the rustlers, assuming they haven't figured out who he is, or holed up somewhere waiting for more help," Will said. "What do you suggest, Jamie?"

"I'll go into town with Drew. Meet with the sheriff, let people know I'm around. Maybe word will get back to Frank and he'll contact us. Either of you know any places in town he'd frequent?"

"Like I said, I didn't get to know him, and never saw him in town. Don't recall him going there much, not even on Saturday nights. Seems strange now that I think on it," Will answered.

"We better let Jake know about him. Don't want Frank to get shot if he does show up back here. I'll send a telegraph to someone I know in Denver who's with the Rangers. That, and Drew's contact with Dunnigan, should help us." Jamie paused and rubbed a hand over his unshaven face. "I heard Grant say he planned to ride out with the men today. What about the women? They okay here on their own?"

"Amanda's fine. Handles a gun, and rides well. Don't really know about Tess or Mrs. Taylor," Will said.

"Tess asked me to help with her shooting. Guess she knows how to handle one but isn't confident like Amanda. I turned her down, pushed her to get Tinder or another ranch hand to help her." Drew still felt bad about refusing her request. He pushed his hands in his pockets and looked down at his dust-covered boots. "Guess I could talk with her today, see if she still wants me to work with her."

A smile passed between Jamie and Will. Drew had always been the shyest of the four brothers, and to their knowledge, had never been serious about anyone. His discomfort conveyed more than he realized.

"I think that's a real good idea, Drew. We need to know the women will be fine if all of us are away." Jamie looked up to see a few men riding toward the ranch house. "Looks like Jake's coming in now. I'll make sure he and Grant know about Frank, and what we suspect. I'll meet you back here in an hour, Drew, so we can head to town."

"Probably a good time for you to speak with Tess, don't you think?" Will smiled at his twin. He turned and started toward the barn, then looked over his shoulder at Drew, who still stood rooted in place. "Might even be able to get in some practice time before you head out."

Will was still chuckling as he entered the barn to grab his gear. It was his shift to watch cattle with the men, but he wanted to make a quick detour towards the Bierdan ranch to see if he could spot Hollis. It'd been several days since he'd seen the man. He needed to catch him alone, force Hollis to confess. Then he'd decide what to do with him.

"Hello, Will."

He turned to see Amanda at the back of the barn, lifting her saddle.

"Amanda."

"Are you heading out? I'll ride with you if you don't mind."

"Tell me you're not thinking of watching the herd. There're plenty of men for that. And besides, your father's going to be out there. Who's going to keep an eye on the ranch? Your mother?"

Amanda placed her hands on her hips and turned toward Will. "Jake and a few of the men are back. They'll watch the place. I want to be out there, where I might be useful."

"You can be more useful here, making sure everyone's safe, and taking care of the chores. And what about Tess? You going to leave her behind?" Will's voice rose along with his concern for Amanda. He just didn't know what else to say to keep her here, safe.

"Tess wouldn't be comfortable riding out with us. Besides, this isn't the kind of work she could do."

"What? Put herself in danger like you want to do?"

They were standing only a foot apart, glaring at each other, neither giving an inch.

"Why are you so insistent I stay here when I'd be more help watching the herd?"

Will stared into her deep blue eyes and tried to calm the fear welling inside him. She was right. He had no right to try and stop her.

"Forget it, Amanda. Go wherever you want." He threw his saddle over his shoulder and started toward the barn door.

"Well then, I choose to go with you."

"No." He didn't look back.

"I'll just follow you."

Will stopped in his tracks, dropped the saddle, and turned to face her. Hands on hips, he looked down for several seconds before raising his eyes to meet hers. Then he started to walk toward her. His arms dropped to his sides as he advanced. One, two, three measured strides, and he stopped inches away. She could feel the heat radiating from his body. He could see the alarm in her eyes, but also the determination not to be intimidated. She raised her chin to glower into eyes that had turned hard as stone.

"You will not, today or ever, while I'm around, place yourself in danger. Not if I can prevent it. This is not something I will discuss further with you, Amanda. Don't push me. You won't like the man you'll see if you do." He stood for several moments, letting her absorb his words, then turned to pick up his gear.

"Why?" Amanda spoke the word in such a soft voice that Will almost missed it. When he didn't respond, but didn't walk away, Amanda moved up behind him and placed a hand on his back. "Why are you acting like this, Will?"

She could sense the struggle within him, feel the muscles in his back tense. He took a couple of deep breaths but did not turn around. Instead, he started forward, and walked away into the early morning sun.

Chapter Eighteen

"Sheriff should be back tomorrow, but perhaps I can help if you can't wait." The deputy eyed the man he'd met the day before and wondered about his business in Cold Creek.

"I'm looking for a man. Frank Alts. He's been working at the Taylor ranch for several months but disappeared a few days ago. You know him?" Jamie had to start some place and with the sheriff out of town the deputy would have to do.

"Sure, I know him. What do you want with him?"

"Just to find him. Mr. Taylor's worried something could've happened. Alts just up and disappeared—left his clothes and extra gear in the bunkhouse. Thought maybe someone in town had seen him."

"I haven't seen him in a few weeks. He's not much for coming to town from what I've heard. I could check around, let people know he's missing."

"Glad for your help, Deputy. Word can be sent to Mr. Taylor if you hear anything." Jamie walked out into a strong wind and looked up and down the main street. He clamped down his hat and walked toward the saloon. It was early, but saloons never closed. Perhaps he'd get lucky.

"What can I get you?" the bartender asked as he set a glass on the bar.

"Just coffee for now and possibly information. You know Frank Alt—works at the Taylor ranch?"

"I know him, but he don't come in here much. Haven't seen him in two, maybe three weeks. Why?"

"He's missing. Left his gear behind." Jamie sipped the hot brew and peered over the rim of his cup at the man across the bar.

"That so? Well, it's strange but not unheard of. Maybe someone was after him and he had to take off in a hurry. I've seen a lot of strange things in my time, if you know what I mean?" The bartender grabbed a towel to wipe down the bar before adding more coffee to Jamie's cup.

"Could be right, but Mr. Taylor wants to find him, so that's what I'm trying to do. I'd appreciate it if you'd send word out to the ranch if you hear anything." Jamie dropped some coins on the counter, four times the amount for coffee, and left the saloon. He tried the gunsmith next, then met Drew at the mercantile.

"Any luck?" Drew asked as Jamie approached.

"Nothing. You?"

"No one's seen him. What now?" Drew grabbed the items he'd purchased and started for the door.

"Head back to the ranch and talk to Grant about places cattle can be kept for long periods, hidden, but with good access to food and water. We need to find the missing cattle and in the process, maybe find Frank."

"Grant will need more men to protect the ranch and horses, keep watch on the herd, and try to locate the stolen cattle. There's just too much ground to cover with the men he has. Another five or six would do it, but where do we find them?" Drew knew his time in Cold Creek was short. Dunnigan wanted him back in Denver in another week, but he wouldn't share that with his brothers—at least not yet.

"That's Taylor's decision to make, not ours." Jamie wished it was his decision. He'd have the extra men hired in a day and positioned about the ranch. His gut told him time was short, that the rustlers would make another move soon.

******

Frank woke to sun burning down on his face. He'd fallen asleep by the stream. The sun was high, and he knew it had to be close to noon. His shoulder throbbed and his back ached, but at least he was alive and near Taylor land. Frank still needed a doctor and food. He couldn't recall the last time he'd eaten but it had to have been several days ago.

Alts pushed up and found it easier to stand than it had been the night before. He looked around and found a long, straight branch that could be used as a walking stick. The ranch house had to be several miles south. For a while he'd be protected by the thick stand of pine, but he'd need to travel over flat pastureland the rest of the way. It would take time but he'd make it to the ranch and in the process decide how to confront, and arrest, Hollis for attempted murder.

An hour passed, maybe two, before Frank came to where he needed to leave the shelter of the trees and start across open land. He stopped to rest and gather his strength. The next few hours would be the worst, but there was no other way to reach the ranch from here. The chances of anyone finding him this far out was slim, so he'd just need to pace himself. He couldn't afford to lose his strength and collapse. If he did, he'd most likely die, and that wasn't an option, not with Aaron waiting for him at home. The thought of his son gave Frank strength. Aaron was the best thing that had ever happened to him and he wouldn't let him down. Not like Aaron's mother had. Frank had no idea where she'd gone and that was fine with him. He hoped she'd never show her face again. Yes, he'd make it through this last assignment and return home, to Denver and to Aaron.

******

"Where next, Jake?" Tinder and the others had been riding on little sleep. Jake had only let them rest three hours before getting them

171

up and back out looking for the missing cattle. He'd told them all what he expected and it didn't include much rest.

"Continue up toward the north pasture. We'll sweep the open areas then check the valleys around the forestlands. Those are the last places I know to hide that large a herd. Something's got to turn up soon." Defeat tinged Jake's voice, a trait uncommon in the long-time foreman, but he was stumped. He had men riding the entire perimeter with nothing to show, not even tracks or any other signs of cattle movement. "Tinder, you go ahead with Johnson while the rest of us spread out to cover more area."

"Sure thing, boss." Tinder spun his horse and Johnson followed, determined to find something to help locate the cattle. Tinder, riding ahead, reined in sharply. "Is that a man?" He approached with caution, then jumped from the saddle when recognition hit. Kneeling beside the figure half buried in the grass, he turned the man over. "My God, it's Alts. Quick, ride back and get Jake. Tell him we found Alts and he's in a bad way." Tinder began to pull the coat, vest, and shirt back. They came away with caked blood and gore, the stink indicating the wound was beginning to fester. He grabbed his canteen and soaked the kerchief he'd pulled from around his neck.

"Frank, you hear me?" Tinder started to clean the wound while urging Frank to respond. "Come on, talk to me." He looked for other injuries, thankful not to find any. He rolled the injured man a little to the side. The bullet had gone clean through. At least they didn't have to worry about digging it out of him. When he rolled him back, a soft moan escaped Frank's lips and his eyes fluttered.

"Frank, can you hear me?"

"Yea, I can hear you." The words were soft, strained. Frank tried to lift his head. "Tinder? What are you doing out here?"

"Trying to save your sorry butt, although I don't quite know why yet. I'm going to help lift your head so you can have some water, but only a sip. Got that?"

"Yea, I got it."

Tinder let a small amount of water trickle down Frank's throat, then eased him back down. Relief washed over him as he saw Jake, Johnson, and the others appear in the distance. "We've got help coming, Frank. Won't be long now."

Jake was the first to arrive. A few minutes later all the men had dismounted to form a circle around Alts.

"Can he travel?" Jake asked Tinder.

Tinder shot a quick look at Frank, but mercifully, the man had passed out. "Far as I can tell. The wound is to his shoulder. It looks like the bullet went through and bleeding's stopped. How do you want to handle this, Jake?"

The foreman looked at all the men before his eyes returned to Tinder. "You're the lightest weight. Let's put Alts in front of you. Can't risk him riding alone. You and Johnson take him back to the ranch, while the rest of us continue north. And be sure to take good care of him. Like I said before, he's a friend of Jamie MacLaren's, and most likely out here with the Rangers. But, keep watch on him. Just because he's with the rangers doesn't mean he ain't dirty."

"Don't worry, Boss, we'll get him back in one piece. I want to find out how Johnny got involved in this mess as much as anyone."

******

"Father, you'd better get out here." Amanda poked her head into Grant's office where he and Jamie were meeting. "It's Tinder and Johnson. Looks like they've got an injured man with them."

"Come on, MacLaren, let's see what's going on." Grant pushed himself out of his chair and led the way outside.

Recognition hit Jamie as soon as the three pulled up to the house. He hurried the short distance down the steps to help Tinder.

"What happened?" Jamie asked.

"Don't know. We found him this way a few miles north, not far from the ranch boundary. He's been shot." Tinder helped carry Alts into the house.

"Johnson," Grant looked at the other ranch hand. "You ride into town and bring the Doc. Don't stop to talk to anyone, understand?"

174

"Yes, sir," Johnson responded and started for town at a crisp gallop.

"Put him in the small room behind Father's office," Amanda directed. "Mother and I will do what we can until the doctor arrives."

"I'm staying," Jamie stated. The tone of his voice told her that his mind was set.

"All right, but let us get him settled before you try to hammer him with questions."

The dried blood formed an adhesion that made Frank's clothing difficult to remove without causing more damage, but the women managed it in just a few minutes. It was obvious to Jamie that they had cared for gunshot wounds before.

"What's going on?" Frank's pain-filled voice broke the silence.

"Frank, it's Jamie MacLaren. You remember me?"

"Yea. What're you doing here?" Frank's words were thick but as his eyes opened Jamie could see recognition.

"My brother, Drew, got me out here when he learned Will had located Hawley. But you already know the man, don't you?" Jamie couldn't keep the slight accusation from his tone.

"Look, I can explain..." Frank started.

The doctor stepped into the room, interrupting them. "There'll be time for questions later. Right now you all need to leave until I've had a chance to check him out. Ladies, I need hot water, clean towels, and some liquor. Immediately"

175

Eleanor nodded.

The doctor set his bag aside, took off his coat, and rolled up his sleeves, but stopped when he realized no one had moved. "All of you, out. Now."

Jamie headed outside when he felt a hand on his arm. He turned to see Amanda staring up at him. "Who's Hawley?"

He considered her question for a moment. It wasn't his place to explain about Will's past. "You'll have to ask Will. It's his story to tell."

Amanda's protest died on her lips at the sound of riders approaching the house. "All right, I'll ask him," she said and hurried outside.

Will and Tinder had their heads together when she walked up. She could hear "Alts," and "gunshot," but that was all before both turned to acknowledge her.

"How's Frank doing?" Will asked.

"Don't know yet but he recognized Jamie. The doctor's with him now, so we'll just have to wait a bit. Tinder, would you give Will and me minute?"

"Sure," Tinder looked at Will. "Johnson and I are going to grab some food then head back out to meet up with Jake. Let me know if you hear anything on Alts."

"I'm going to ride back out with Tinder, Amanda. What is it you want to talk about?"

"Who's Hawley?"

Hawley's name coming from Amanda was the last thing Will expected. Besides his family, no one at the Taylor ranch knew that

176

name or the true reason for Will coming to Cold Creek. "Why do you ask?" His terse tone and rigid stance told Amanda this was not going to be an easy conversation.

"Jamie mentioned the name to Frank. Your brother said I'd have to ask you if I wanted answers," she paused a moment, hoping Will would explain, but continued when he remained silent. "So, who is he?"

"Just a man. A man who leaves death and misery wherever he goes. He's not someone you ever want to get to know. The man is pure evil." Will grabbed Justice's reins and turned to follow Tinder.

"That's not good enough. I want to know who he is to you and why Jamie would mention his name."

He stopped. His words were soft but hard as granite. "The man is my business. Not yours, not Jamie's, or anyone else's. I'll not talk about him with you." He tried to walk away again, but the next words stopped him.

"Does he have anything to do with your wife?"

Will closed his eyes. He didn't want to talk about Hawley, nor about Emily and her brutal death. His goal was simple. Find the man and kill him. If it meant his own life, then so be it. At least he'd finally be at peace, knowing he'd done what he could to avenge his wife.

"Will?"

He felt his chest tighten at the memories as well as the bone-deep ache that was always just a thought away. In one fluid move, he mounted his horse. He debated for just a moment before turning his pain-filled eyes toward Amanda. "He murdered her."

Amanda's heart clenched as she absorbed his words. She watched in silence as Will turned his back and rode off, taking the rest of his secrets with him.

Chapter Nineteen

"Once more, Tess." Drew stood behind Tess as she loaded the six-shooter Grant had given her a few years earlier. She'd wanted one of the smaller guns available in town but Grant had said she needed to get used to a real gun that would provide real protection. It was hard for her to handle, but she was determined to prove she could help if there was trouble.

"The same target?" She started to aim at the old bucket filled with rocks he'd set on a stack of deadfall a few yards away.

"Same target. You're going to shoot at it until it's filled with holes."

Drew watched her take aim and fire. The bullet grazed the side of the bucket but didn't pierce it. "Again, Tess." They'd been at it for over an hour and he knew she was tired. He also knew trouble could come at any time and she needed to be ready.

The next shot went straight through the target. "I got it!" Tess's broad smile made Drew chuckle. He couldn't fault her enthusiasm even if her aim needed work.

"Good shot. Now empty the rest of the gun into that bucket and we'll finish up." He watched as she continued to aim and fire. "You've done real well today, but we should practice again tomorrow. That is, if you're up for it." To Drew's surprise, he was actually enjoying his time with her. She didn't get frustrated and wouldn't give up.

"Of course I want to practice again tomorrow. I'll practice until I get as good as Amanda." The last was said as she raised the pistol once more and aimed. She hit the bucket three of the next five shots, the last one toppling the bucket to the ground. Her eyes danced with pride. Not bad for someone who hadn't shot in years.

"Okay, that's good for now." Drew reached for the gun, checked the cylinder, and handed it back to Tess. "Let's get back to the house. I want to see if Jake or Will found any more cattle."

It was a short ride. The sky was clear, but that could change in an instant. The Colorado mountain area was notorious for fast mood swings that would blanket the area with rain or a dusting of snow with little warning. It was one of the reasons Tess loved it so much. It was wild and unpredictable, two traits the young woman wished she possessed.

"How long will you be staying, Drew?" she asked as the house came into view.

"Anxious for me to leave?"

"No." She clamped down on her impulse to ask him to stay longer—just to help at the ranch, of course. Her eyes moved from him to the house ahead. She didn't want him to know how much she enjoyed his company. "I just wondered if you'd stay until the missing cattle are found."

"That so?" Drew watched her squirm a little in her saddle and wondered if she wanted him to stay for reasons other than finding the herd.

"Well, yes. I know we can use the help and with your brothers here..." her voice trailed off as a rider approached. Will pulled Justice alongside Drew's horse and tipped his hat at Tess.

"Heading to the west border, then riding north to see if I missed anything," Will informed the pair. "They found Frank—Doc's with him now. I'll be back in a few hours." He nudged his horse into a gallop and was a good distance away before Drew made his decision.

"Tess, I'm going with him. Let Jamie know, will you?" He started off at a brisk pace to catch his brother.

******

"You think the cattle are still in the canyon, north of the ranch?" Grant asked Frank. The doctor had made quick work of the wound, declared that the man would live, but admonished Grant and Jamie to give him time to rest. That hadn't happened.

"Don't see how they could move. Where would they go unless they started driving them to Slider Junction? That's where they talked of taking them before Hollis shot me." Frank struggled to a sitting position. "Another

181

thing. I think there's someone else involved. Chet kept referring to 'the boss,' and having to meet with him."

"Any idea who the man might be?" Jamie asked.

"None. He never mentioned his name or if he's from around here. You want to hand me that water, Jamie?"

Grant walked to the window to peer out at the ranch he'd built with his own sweat over many long years. He wouldn't let anyone steal from him. He sure hoped the man involved wasn't who he suspected. It had been years, but grudges die slowly, especially between two proud men.

"I can show you where the cattle are, but think real hard about it, Grant," Frank said. "Hollis is determined to take your remuda with him and he's a man who doesn't give up what he wants. The horses are here. My guess is they'll come for them soon, and anything else they can grab. Maybe tonight, maybe tomorrow—but they'll come."

Grant considered Frank's words. The loss of the cattle would be hard, but losing the remuda would set them back even more. "Tinder and Johnson already left to find Jake and search the north border. Jamie, you mind going after them? Tell Jake I want to stop the search until we can make sure the extra horses are safe. Once everyone is back, I'll send three or four to find the location Frank gives us and keep watch on the cattle." He turned as the door to his office opened and Eleanor walked in with Tess.

"Will and Drew rode toward the west border. They didn't tell Tess how long they'd be gone," his wife informed the three men.

"The west border, huh? Toward Bierdan's ranch. Well, I guess we'll just have to send someone after them," Grant said.

"I'll leave now," Jamie volunteered. "How long since they left, Tess?"

"Not long at all. Drew and I met Will as he was riding out. They couldn't be more than a few miles from here."

That was the last Jamie heard as he dashed out the front door to follow his brothers. He had a bad feeling about all of this, and it wasn't just the missing cattle. His gut told him this would not end well.

******

"Amanda, are you out here?" Tess headed off to find her sister. *Sister*. The word sounded so strange but at the same time so right. A smiled curled her lips as she walked around to the back of the house. Sure enough, Amanda was sitting on their old swing, idly rocking back and forth as if nothing extraordinary was happening.

"Amanda, I've been looking for you." One look told Tess something was wrong. "What is it? Are you all right?"

Amanda paused the swing to look up at Tess. "His wife was murdered."

"Murdered? Whose wife? You're not making any sense."

"Will's wife. Some man named Hawley murdered her and he's somewhere around here. That's why Will came to Cold Creek. I'm sure of it." She continued to rock at a slow pace. She still felt the pain of his words and wished she hadn't pushed him so hard.

"I didn't know he had been married," Tess said. "Was it a long time ago?"

"He hasn't said. In fact, if I hadn't pressed it, he wouldn't have told me about Hawley, either." She realized how little she knew about their ranch hand. But the lack of information didn't seem to stop her rebellious heart from wanting him. "Will rode out to find him. I think he means to kill the man."

"Drew went with him, and Jamie is following. Grant...our father...wants everyone back at the house. They think the rustlers plan to come after the horses and he wants all the men here. It's Hollis, Amanda."

"Hollis?"

"Frank said Chet Hollis is the one leading the rustlers."

The news should've shocked Amanda, but for whatever reason, it all seemed to fit. She'd known the man wasn't what he pretended to be, but she hadn't thought of him as a thief.

Something in Amanda's brain clicked and she jumped from the swinging seat. "Wait, you said Frank told Father it was Hollis? But he also spoke with Jamie about a man named

Hawley. Did he mention that name to Father?"

"Not that I heard. Why?" Tess got the words out just as Amanda dashed for the back door of the house.

"Father!" she said as she flew into the office.

Grant and Eleanor turned, alarm written on each face. "Amanda, what is it?"

"Where is he?" Amanda looked around the office.

"Who?"

"Frank, where is he?" She couldn't control the panic that had set in when the pieces began to connect. She hoped the fear she felt wasn't justified and that the man they called Hollis wasn't Hawley, the man Will sought.

"Why, he's upstairs, dear. He needed a bed, so..." Eleanor began, but her daughter was already out of the room, running past a surprised Tess, and flying up the stairs. Grant and Eleanor recovered in an instant to follow Amanda.

"Is it true?" Frank's door burst open and he looked up to see a red-faced and agitated woman staring at him. At least he'd pulled the covers up and wasn't completely exposed.

"Is what true, ma'am?" He would've laughed except for the pure panic he saw in her eyes.

"Are Chet Hollis and this Hawley fellow the same man?"

He didn't know where this conversation was heading, but it didn't seem good. "Well, now..." he began.

"Is he?" Amanda's voice rose as she walked closer to the bed, arms folded across her chest, cheeks as flushed as if she been sitting in front of a raging fire.

"Yes, ma'am. Chet Hollis and Chad Hawley are the same man."

Grant, Eleanor, and Tess had been standing at the open door, listening, but without a bit of understanding. They watched as Amanda's arms fell to her sides and she sat down on the edge of the bed to stare at the floor.

"Amanda," Grant's voice penetrated her thoughts and she looked up to see the concern on her father's face. "What's this about?"

"Hollis and Hawley are the same man, Father." At Grant's continued look of confusion, Amanda explained. "Will came to Cold Creek to look for a man named Hawley. The man who murdered Will's wife. He's going to kill him, Father, or at least try. Isn't that right, Mr. Alts?"

Frank was uncomfortable discussing Will's past and long sought vengeance. He didn't know what MacLaren had planned with Hawley, but he knew it wasn't good. "I don't honestly know for sure, ma'am."

"But you know Hawley killed Will's wife?" Grant asked while Eleanor tried to comfort Amanda.

"If Hollis and Hawley are the same man, then yes, Mr. Taylor. From all the information I know, Hawley murdered Wills' wife, five years ago near Fire Mountain. She was pregnant at the time. MacLaren took it real hard—never got over it and has sought vengeance ever since."

The room was silent, each person hearing the words but unable to respond. What kind of man would murder a pregnant young woman?

"Will rode out to find him, Father. Hollis works for Bierdan, and that's where Will was heading." Amanda's voice was flat and laced with defeat.

"Drew's with him, and Jamie may have found them by now. Surly they'll talk sense into him. Don't you think so, Grant?" Eleanor asked as she sat next to Amanda, arms around her daughter.

"God knows I'd like to think so, but if it were me, God knows I'd be doing the same thing as Will." His words sent a chill through the room.

"Well, we'll just go after them and make sure nothing happens," Tess said from her position just inside the bedroom.

"No," Grant, Frank, and Eleanor replied at the same time.

"At least you're not going, Tess, and neither is Amanda." Grant stopped at the sound of horses. "That must be Jake. I'll go talk with him and we'll figure this out." He turned to Amanda. "I'll do whatever I can to

187

make sure he's all right. That's all I can promise." He bent down to place a kiss on his daughter's forehead before leaving to find his foreman.

Chapter Twenty

It was dark by the time Jamie caught up with his brothers. They'd ridden to the west property line all right, but instead of veering north, they'd made their way toward the Bierdan ranch, trying to find Hollis. It was getting late but Will and Drew continued their vigil. The killer was nowhere in sight. Neither heard Jamie behind them until a gun being cocked got their attention. Each started to pull their own weapons.

"I could've been Hawley, you know," Jamie's aggravated voice pierced the night air. "Only you'd both be dead now."

Drew and Will stood from their stooped positions behind a group of dead trees and holstered their Colts.

"What the hell are you doing here, and who's watching the ranch?" Will snarled at him.

"I could ask you the same thing, but I already know the answer," Jamie shot back. He, too, holstered his gun. "This isn't the way, Will. Let Frank or another lawman arrest Hawley. He'll go to trial, be found guilty, and hang. He tried to kill Frank and that alone will get him executed. Hawley is already a walking dead man. Don't make it worse."

For the first time in years, Will thought there might be an alternative to killing Hollis. Maybe Jamie, Drew, Niall, and most everyone else who knew of the tragedy were right. He'd found the man, could lead the Rangers to him, and would stay to watch him hang. It had been five long years, and it was almost over.

"Maybe you are right, along with everyone else, Jamie. I'll go back to the ranch with you and talk with Frank. I can't promise anything, but if we can bring him in to hang, I'll go with it. But if Hawley runs, I'll be going after him."

"That's all I can ask." Jamie replied and let out a deep breath. At least it was a start. Now they just had to find and arrest Hawley before he killed again.

******

"Everyone here, Del?" Hollis glanced around. It looked like all the men had arrived. Chet had met with the boss earlier to finalize tonight's raid. The boss would meet them in Slider Junction in three days to arrange transport of the cattle to Denver. The brands had been changed and there were enough men guarding the herd. The men here could ride to the Taylor ranch to steal the remuda. Hollis chuckled as he pictured the surprise on Grant's face when he realized his prized horses were gone.

"They're all here, Chet."

"All right, men, listen up. We'll split into two groups when we get a mile from the

190

ranch. Del will lead his group straight to the horses from the end opposite the house, and I'll lead a group to make sure no one from the Taylor ranch comes after them. Those with me have to be prepared to kill, and I mean even the women, if they start shooting at us. We'll make no exceptions. Everyone with me?" Chet watched the quiet gathering. All heads nodded. He'd worked for months to find the right men—greedy men who lacked a conscience. "We'll meet the others at the canyon and head out tonight, with horses and cattle, for Slider Junction. Be prepared for no rest the next three days. We're almost done. Let's go."

Several miles later Hollis and his men pulled up and split into two groups. It was late, and from their location they could see lights still burning in the house. Hollis didn't care, and truth be told, thought this might be the best way to end it with MacLaren. Kill the man like he should have done five years before.

Del took off around one side of the property, making sure to keep far enough away so that anyone in the bunkhouse couldn't hear the horses. He saw the corral with the remuda and signaled his men to spread out. Del hoped Chet was in position. There'd be no better time than now. He waited for the signal.

******

Ten hand-picked men accompanied Chet to the house. He wasn't taking any chances that the MacLaren men would walk out of this alive. His message to them had been clear—nobody was to leave the house. Five men were sent to guard the bunkhouse and barn area. He sent two more to the back of the house, leaving Chet and three other men to guard the front. Everyone was in place.

Hollis pulled a cheroot from his vest pocket and lit it. He took one draw and turned toward the horse corral. He put the cheroot to his mouth again, this time taking a long, slow drag on the thin cigar. A bright red glow burned in the moonless night. The signal to proceed had been given.

Del saw it and gave another signal to release the gate. Just as his man readied to open the corral, a loud voice boomed from a few yards away.

"I wouldn't touch that gate, son, unless you have a wish to die tonight."

The young rustler turned and drew his gun but he couldn't see anyone.

"Don't do it!" another voice warned, but it had no effect. The thief spun around again, and along with several others began to shoot wildly into the dark. Not a minute later four of the seven rustlers lay dead, including Del Wiley. They'd ridden into a trap. The last of the rustlers spun their horses away from the gunfire and bloodshed, determined to get away. Grant's men started running, keeping low and staying close to the corral fence.

Gunshots from the house grabbed the men's attention.

"Jake," Grant yelled. "Take Tinder and a few others and follow those low-lifes. Stop them before they get into the mountain country."

"Will do, boss," Jake and his men started out after the remaining thieves.

Grant and two men continued toward the house. He'd left two others inside along with Alts and hoped they were able to hold off the other robbers a little longer.

******

Everyone in the house was in place. Amanda and Tess were in the living room with Gus, one of their men. Another ranch hand was in the office, Frank was upstairs, and Eleanor had just finished hiding Joey and Maria behind a trap door in the pantry with strict instructions not to come out, no matter what they heard.

Gus looked over at Amanda, crouched by the window. "Miss Amanda, get down and give me that gun."

"I can handle this gun just fine, Gus, and you know it," she whispered back just as a bullet crashed through a window and slammed into the man's shoulder.

"Mother! It's Gus, he's bleeding." Eleanor dropped the rifle she held and ran to their long-time employee. She tore some fabric from the bottom of her chemise and pressed it into the wound.

"I've got him, Amanda. Please stay down," her mother pleaded.

A shot rang out from the second floor and a loud crash was heard behind the house. They hadn't been sure that Frank could handle a gun with his injury but he'd assured them they were wrong. Now they could hear him moving towards a front bedroom.

Another shot echoed through the night, then another bullet pierced the glass in the office. The women heard a moan. The other ranch hand had been hit. A moment later, Eleanor was at his side, trying to stop the bleeding from a graze to the head that bled a lot, but the wound didn't appear as serious as Gus's.

All the women could do was stay low and try to hold off the attackers until Grant and the other men could reach them. They heard the shots from the horse corral and realized help might come later than they'd hoped.

"What can I do?" Tess crawled from behind the divan, a gun in one hand and a box of shells in the other.

"Oh Lord," was all Eleanor could get out before another blast of gunfire ripped through the windows. "Stay down, Tess. Your father will be here soon to help us."

"No, I can do this. I've been practicing with Drew for just this kind of attack. I won't sit back and wait for them to come into the house." Tess's fingers shook as she loaded shells into the pistol, but Eleanor saw the determination in the young woman's face and understood this was something Tess had to do.

All three women's heads snapped toward the front door at the sound of someone just outside.

"Come out, MacLaren. I know you're in there."

Amanda recognized Chet Hollis's voice and cringed. He was after the horses, and Will. She raised herself to the window and peered out. Hollis and another man stood flush against the outside wall. She could just make out the outlines of a few other men near the bunkhouse. She hoped her Father saw them, but she couldn't wait to find out. Amanda couldn't get a shot off at Hollis but she might be able to hit one of the men at the bunkhouse. She aimed and fired at the same instant a shot from upstairs rang out. Two of Hollis' men crumbled to the ground. *How many more?* Amanda wondered.

Chet yelled, "You can't hold out forever in there. Come out, MacLaren, and we'll let everyone else go. Just you and me, the way it should be." Three bullets riddled the front door and a loud blow made the door shudder. Amanda realized he was trying to break it down.

"Will's gone, Chet. He took off hours ago and no one's seen him. Take your men and leave before anyone else dies," she shouted through a shattered window.

195

"Ah, Miss Taylor. How nice to hear your voice. Why don't you come out and we can talk this over? You and me," Hollis called back and waved to the remaining men near the bunkhouse to start moving toward the barn and house. It had become clear the bunkhouse was empty and that Taylor had men spread out around the horse corral. It had been a trap but he still might be able to get away with the one thing he prized the most—Amanda Taylor.

"Don't you even consider it, Amanda," her mother whispered as she crawled toward her.

The women heard another gun blast. "I got one!" an excited shout came from the office. Tessa had taken a shot and it had paid off.

Amanda took a quick look outside and saw that another man lay prone between the house and bunkhouse. "Good shot, Tess. We need to figure out how many more men Hollis has with him. Can you see any from the office?"

"I just saw another one run from the bunkhouse but I couldn't get him," Tess replied.

"Well, four are down, but how many are left?"

"Seven. There are still seven men," Frank's words drifted down the stairs as he made his way to the living room. "One out back, three by the barn, and three out front."

Amanda raised her head once more to look out the window. No one. The front porch was empty. "They're gone," she said and looked at Frank.

"Not gone, just changed their positions. The shooting has stopped by the corral, so my guess is Grant and some others are making their way to the house. Hollis or one of his men probably spotted them and are preparing to pick them off. I'll need to get outside, see if I can help," Frank's tone was matter-of-fact as he reloaded his pistol.

Frank made his way through the kitchen to the back door and looked out. He spotted one of the robbers partially hidden behind a tree about five yards away. He leveled his pistol and waited. Five seconds, ten seconds passed before the man leaned out. One shot and the man slumped to the ground. That left six. Frank scanned the area once more, caught slight movement, and saw the silhouette of a man making his way behind the woodpile, toward his fallen comrade. Curses spewed from the robber when he turned the body over. Frank knew the rustler was dead.

Frank took aim again. His shot was wide and his target leapt behind a large tree. A blast peppered the back door, then another. A single shot broke the glass above the sink. It sounded like another outlaw had joined the first. Frank heard feet pounding on dry ground and realized they were rushing the house. He stood to the side of the back door, aimed directly at the entrance and waited. It only took seconds for the first man to kick the door open, but a bullet from Frank had him on the ground before he had a chance to cross the threshold. Frank moved fast, centered his gun on the second man and fired. The rustler slumped to the ground. That still left four.

Frank made his way outside and around the house, trying to get a good view of the barn. Gunfire reverberated through the night, followed by moans, but he had no idea if it was a robber or Taylor man who'd gone down.

"They got Tuck, Grant." Hal, the one remaining ranch hand crouched beside his boss behind a row of barrels next to the barn. Before Grant had a chance to reply the men heard movement behind them, and turned to see two rifles pointed at them.

"Don't try something stupid, Mr. Taylor. I'm not ready to rid the world of your presence, at least not quite yet," Chet smirked. "Drop your guns and we'll reunite you with your lovely daughter and wife."

"What's this about, Hollis?" Grant glared at the man who held him hostage.

"If you think about it hard enough I believe you'll figure it out."

"It's not just about the cattle or horses, is it?" Grant was trying to stall, hoping the MacLarens might make it back in time to stop the massacre.

"Cattle, horses, land, people. It's about all of it, Taylor. My boss believes you stole something from him years ago, and now he wants it back."

"Bierdan," Grant said and resigned himself to the fact that his guess had been right.

"That's right—Bierdan. Guess you shouldn't have crossed him. The man's not one to forgive and forget. Now, turn around and start for the house." Hollis raised the gun to indicate their conversation had ended.

Frank saw Grant and Hal walk from around the barn, then cursed when he saw Hollis and another man following. At the same instant, two more of Chet's men emerged from the barn to join their boss. Four men using the other two as shields. Frank had to come up with something fast, but what?

Chapter Twenty-One

The MacLaren brothers were still a mile from the ranch house when they heard the distinct sound of gunfire. A quick look between them was all it took before each horse began to fly across the open land.

Will reached the edge of the fence first and reined Justice to a stop. Seconds later, Drew and Jamie pulled up beside him.

"Shit, it's Hollis, and he's got Grant and Hal. I can see three I don't recognize—must be with Hollis," Will ground out as fear began to tighten his chest. "The women must still be in the house with Frank."

"We can't wait until Hollis gets the women to come out. We need to move fast, surprise them before they claim more hostages." Jamie's old life kicked in as his mind quickly assessed what needed to be done.

"What do you want us to do, Jamie?" Drew asked.

"Drew, you move in from the left, Will from the right. I'll go straight in and take out Hollis first, then the man next to him. You two okay taking out the others?" Jamie was already checking his pistol.

"Hollis is mine. I'll kill the bastard," Will said with finality. Jamie and Drew looked at each other but didn't protest.

"All right. I'll take the man next to Hollis and the tall, slim one. Drew, you take the short one to the far right," Jamie said. "All right. Let's move up as close as possible, get in position, then move fast. There won't be time for a second shot or Hollis might kill Grant. First shot's got to hit the mark." Will and Drew, nodded and the three moved forward.

******

"Ladies," Hollis called into the house, "I'd suggest you make your way outside before we have to rid you of one more man."

Eleanor, Amanda, and Tess looked through broken glass to see Grant standing, arms slack at his sides, facing the house.

"They'll kill Father and Hal if we don't go out," Amanda's face reflected her misery.

"They'll kill all of us either way. We know who they are—they're not going to let any of us live through this," Eleanor replied. "But, we can't just stay here and take the chance." Resignation laced her voice.

"I think we should shoot them. They'll never think we'd take the chance," Tess offered.

Amanda put an arm around her sister. "That may be right, Tess, but we can't take the chance. Our aim just isn't that good."

"Well then, let's go," Eleanor motioned for the others to put the guns on a nearby table. She looked around the living room that had been her home for over twenty years and wondered if she'd ever see it again or sit with Grant at night to share their day. She and her husband had plans. This wasn't the way their lives were supposed to end. Eleanor reached out to grab the door handle but the sound of rapid gunfire stopped her.

The women moved to the closest window and looked out. What they saw shocked all three. Hollis and his men lay on the ground while Grant and Hal stood motionless and stared at the bodies around them.

"What on earth?" Eleanor asked no one in particular and ran outside. Amanda and Tess followed, but stopped as Jamie and Will rode up and dismounted.

Neither said a word to anyone, but walked to each body and kicked it to confirm each man was dead.

Hollis was the only one who stirred. Blood streamed from his slack lips and pooled on the ground. His eyes began to glaze. He recognized the man glaring down at him—Will MacLaren. *I lost and MacLaren won.* It was his last thought before his heart stopped.

Will stared at the man who had ruined his life and watched as the life flowed out of him. It was over. The long search had ended and the vengeance he'd sought for his wife had been realized. It was a justifiable and righteous death, but too quick for a man as evil as Hollis.

"What happened?" Jamie walked up to Will to peer down at the object of his brother's five-year journey.

202

"He's dead," Will looked at Jamie with confused eyes.

"I'm asking about Drew. He didn't get his man and he's not here. Did you see him after the men fell?"

Will looked around as fear gripped him. "No!" he roared and ran to mount Justice. Jamie was right behind on Rebel. They wasted no time finding the spot where Drew had taken cover. Their horses had barely stopped when they each jumped off and ran to the body of their brother.

"God, no!" Will's agonized cry pierced the night sky as he fell to his knees beside his twin. Drew lay prone on the ground but was breathing. Jamie crouched on the other side as they gently examined him. There was blood around his waist and hips, and down his legs.

Jamie pulled back Drew's clothing to expose a wound where a bullet had ripped into the right hip. It appeared that the bullet was still lodged in his body. Will tore off his shirt and applied pressure to the wound. Jamie grabbed his canteen to wash the blood away.

"I'll go back and have Grant send someone for the doctor. I'll bring back the wagon. Are you going to be okay here for a while?" Jamie asked Will.

"Yes, I'll be fine. Just hurry."

Within seconds Jamie was riding away as fast as Rebel could run. He could see Amanda and Tess start to run toward him with blankets but he waived them off.

"We found him. He's hurt, bad," Jamie dismounted and ran to Grant. "Send for the doctor. And we need a buckboard."

Grant never hesitated but instructed Hal to ride hard to get the doc. Jamie, Grant, and Amanda took care of the buckboard while Tess grabbed water, towels, and whiskey to go with the blankets she already carried.

"I'll get a place ready for him," Eleanor yelled as she rushed into the house.

"I'm coming with you, Jamie," Frank said but Jamie held him off.

"Stay here. Help Eleanor with whatever she needs."

"You drive, Father," Amanda said and jumped in the back of the wagon with Tess while Jamie mounted Rebel.

Will, waiting for the wagon, continued to apply pressure to the wound. "Drew, can you hear me?" He thought he'd get no response, but heard a slight moan. "Drew, I'm here. You're going to be okay."

"What happened?" Drew asked, then winced from the sudden onslaught of pain. Recall came soon afterwards. "God, wherever that bastard hit me, it sure hurts."

Will would've laughed if his brother hadn't been in so much pain. "You remember?"

"Only that I was about ready to pull the trigger and pain shot through me—from behind. I remember falling to the ground, then nothing."

Will looked up to see Jamie on Rebel, and Grant driving the wagon. Thank God, they

204

weren't far from the house. Drew had taken up a position about a hundred-fifty yards out—a sizable distance with a rifle, but he was a good shot, better than most men.

Amanda and Tess jumped from the wagon. Each loaded their arms with supplies, ran to Drew, and dropped to their knees.

"How's he doing, Will?" Tess asked in a soft, calm voice but her eyes reflected the concern all of them felt.

"He's going to live," Drew replied in a strained voice.

"Good, you're conscious. Do you remember anything?" Tess continued to speak to him in a soothing voice while she removed Will's shirt from the wound and rinsed it with water. Amanda handed her the bottle of whiskey. "Drew, this is going to hurt but I don't know how long it will take for the doctor to get here and we need to stop any infection. Okay?"

"Wait. Give me some of that whiskey before you waste it on my wound." The demand made Tess smile and helped the others relax.

Jamie helped turn him on his side while Will held his head. Tess started to move the bottle to his lips when Drew snatched from her. "I can do it," he said, and poured a generous amount of the golden liquid down his throat. "Okay, now I'm ready."

Everyone watched as Tess poured whiskey on the wound. Drew winced but otherwise remained motionless. She signaled for

205

Amanda to hand her a towel and began to clean the wound with more alcohol. Drew sucked in his breath but again his body was still.

"We need to get you in the wagon. It'll hurt, but there's no help for it," Tess warned him. Three strong sets of arms wrapped around Drew and lifted. He didn't make a sound. Amanda glanced at Tess but the younger woman shook her head. The men placed Drew on blankets in the back of the wagon and Amanda covered him with additional ones.

"You girls hold him secure during the ride back. Won't take long," Grant said and slapped the reins.

******

"How is he, Doc?" Will asked when the doctor emerged from the downstairs bedroom where they'd placed Drew. As he'd done with Frank, the doctor had shooed everyone from the room, except Eleanor. This time he had her stay. Will glanced at her and his stomach plummeted. The look on her face was grave, devoid of the encouraging smile he'd expected.

All the others had crowded around Will to hear the news.

"It's not good, I'm afraid," the doc said and a noticeable tension over-took the room.

"What do you mean?" Jamie's frustration was directed at the Doc.

"I'm getting to that, young man," the doctor replied and Jamie backed off. "The bullet is still lodged in his back. I don't know how close it is to his spinal cord but it can't be far. I can do my best to remove it without causing further damage, but there are risks. What worries me is that he can't feel anything in his legs—nothing from his waist down. I need to get the bullet out to stop infection but there's a risk that if there's already damage to the spine, removing the bullet could make it worse."

The room fell silent. Will ran a hand through his already disheveled hair and Jamie walked to the living room and dropped into a nearby chair. Everyone followed.

"You boys want to be alone, talk about this with the doc?" Grant asked.

The brothers looked at Grant but neither said a word. Finally, Jamie cleared the catch in his voice and responded. "No, we'd appreciate it if you'd stay. Help us talk through this. Not sure that either Will or I are thinking too straight right now."

"You okay with that, son?" Grant asked Will, who just nodded his agreement.

"How much time before these two have to make a decision, Doc?" Grant asked.

"Well now, I'd like to do this soon, before there's more damage. Within an hour at the latest."

"Eleanor, would you mind getting us all some coffee? Might help us think better."

Grant smiled at his wife as she turned for the kitchen. He motioned everyone to have a seat.

Will slammed the flat of his hand into a wall. "It's my fault." No one said a word, just let him get it out. "I told Drew over and over that I didn't want him here, that I could handle this on my own. Now this." The agony in his voice brought tears to Amanda's eyes.

Jamie walked to his brother, and placed a hand on his shoulder "He was here because that's what he wanted. It wasn't your decision to make. He knew the danger and he chose to accept it. If you were in his place, would you have stayed away?"

Will contemplated Jamie's words. "No, I would've come anyway."

"All right, then, let's talk about this decision that must be made," Jamie said to everyone. "Doc, how good are you as a surgeon? Do people live or die under your hand?"

The doctor was taken aback only a little, then a smile curved his lips. "That's an excellent question, young man. The truth is, I haven't had to remove a bullet quite like this one in a long time. Not since the War when I was a surgeon for the Union Army. But at that time, I did pretty well. Course, they were running the injured through quicker than I liked, but that was war. Taking my time, the clean conditions we have here, and Eleanor's help, I'd give your brother a fifty-fifty chance of no additional damage. That's the best I can tell you." The doctor sipped at the hot brew Eleanor handed him.

"And infection if the bullet stays inside Drew?"

"That's the critical issue here. Leaving the bullet will most likely cause infection which could lead to death. Taking it out will give your brother a much better chance to live. It may cause more damage—increase the lack of feeling or worse—but the chances that he'll live are much better."

Will looked to Grant. "What do you think?"

Grant didn't hesitate. "Your brother is a smart man, an attorney. He's got good experience and mighty fine connections. Seems to me it'd be best to be alive and practicing law, then dead from infection. Besides, we don't know if the paralysis is permanent or temporary, right Doc?"

"That's true, Grant. Truth is, we might not know for several weeks or months. Some people do have injuries that heal with time and rest. Your brother might be one of those."

Jamie and Will took in the words of both men, then spoke in soft tones between themselves. Will ran another hand through his hair as Jamie kept talking, but it didn't take long for them to agree.

"We'll go for the surgery, Doctor," Will said with finality. Jamie squeezed his brother's shoulder, then sat down next to Tess.

"All right, boys. I think you've made a wise decision. He's out from the laudanum so now's a good time to get started. Eleanor, you up for this?"

"I'd be honored to help that boy, Doctor. Just tell me what to do." The two disappeared into the back bedroom.

Chapter Twenty-Two

"How do you want to handle this, Grant?" Will asked the day after his brother's surgery. Drew had come through fine, but the paralysis remained. It didn't seem to be any worse, and at least the bullet was gone. But his mood was something no one wanted to be around for long. He was on heavy doses of laudanum and was half-witted much of time. Grant's decision to go after the cattle, then focus on finding the man who'd shot Drew sounded real good to Will and Jamie.

"Tinder just got back an hour ago, but according to him, Jake and the rest of my men are keeping watch on where the rustlers are holding the missing cattle. He can take us to them. It'll be Tinder, you two, plus Frank and I riding out with the other men. Damn fool insists on going even with his injured shoulder. Tinder estimates only ten rustlers for all that cattle. We've got fifteen so that's good odds," Grant paused to toss out his tepid coffee. "Can't wait any longer if we hope to get them all back."

"We're ready when you are." Jamie had expected Grant's decision. It made sense. Stalling would serve no purpose.

"Is everyone ready to go, Will?" Amanda walked up to Justice and stroked the long, sleek, black neck of the stallion. He was a magnificent animal, much like his owner. She'd stopped denying her feelings and had come to terms about her deep affection for Will. She was in love with him.

"Looks like it. Hope to be back by nightfall, with the cattle, and perhaps the men who took them," Will replied. "You'll watch over Drew for us, right?" He was torn. He needed to go help recover the cattle but wanted to stay in case his brother needed him.

"Of course. Tess and I will take turns checking on him. You don't need to worry."

Amanda and Tess watched the men ride out. Their father had refused to let either go along and warned each there'd be severe consequences if they tried to follow.

"I guess I'll go check on our patient," Tess began to turn toward the house, but stopped. "I don't believe he's accepted that he's paralyzed, at least for now. When he's lucid, he focuses on what the Doc said about the bullet not hitting his spine. He's sure he'll recover in a few days and start back for Denver." Tess folded her hands in front of her. "It could be temporary. I'm just worried how he'll do if the paralysis lasts for weeks or months. Or, if he's never able to walk again. He's a good man, Amanda. It's just not right." Anger, and perhaps something else, laced her words.

Amanda walked up and pulled her sister into her arms. She could feel Tess's body tremble and realized the young woman felt much more for Drew than she'd let on.

"It's in God's hands now, Tess. All we can do is be here for him and pray that he regains the use of his legs. It's going to be a long recovery whether he walks again or not. But, like Father said, Drew has education and skills that can be used whether he stands or sits. That's a lot more than most men have. He's strong. I know he'll get through this." She hugged Tess tighter then stepped back. "Come on. I'll go with you to check on the grizzly bear inside."

******

"Let's ride out, men. I expect Taylor will find this spot soon enough and we need to be long on our way before that happens." Gordon Bierdan had no choice but to lead the drive to Slider Junction. Hollis and Wiley were both dead. There wasn't anyone else he trusted to get the cattle to the railroad. His partner in Denver wouldn't be happy with the change, but there was no choice.

He knew he'd screwed up and shot the wrong MacLaren. He had spotted them the day before as they surveyed his ranch and realized they'd figured most of it out. At least he was sure they knew his men were involved in the rustling. Gordon followed them when they rode off, but held back when he heard the

213

shooting at the Taylor place. He'd tried to get in position to bring down two of them but wasn't fast enough, so Gordon decided he could at least get the one who was after Hollis. Now he realized the wrong man had fallen. It was a critical mistake. He knew Will wouldn't stop until he found the man who had shot his brother.

Gordon rode his horse to the front of the herd and motioned that the drive had begun. They'd have to take the cattle through a narrow gorge that few men knew about. Grant and maybe a handful of men besides himself had ever seen it. It would be slow moving as the animals would need to go through two or three at a time, but once on the other side, it was a clear expanse of open land for miles. That's where they'd meet up with the chuck wagon and extra horses. The men at the back had been instructed to close the narrow opening when they passed through. Once closed, anyone who followed would be required to ride a full day around the mountain to get to the open plain. The cattle would be almost to Slider Junction by then.

Bierdan rode through first and motioned for his men to drive the cattle forward. Only six or seven head had passed through when a shot rang out. It hit the ground not five feet from where Gordon sat atop his horse. Dust flew up and the cattle began to panic.

"You're through, Gordon. Don't push that herd any farther. My men have orders to open fire if any more cattle come through that pass." Grant's deep voice echoed through the narrow canyon.

Gordon circled his horse and peered up at the ridge above. Nothing. He had no doubt Grant had men stationed above and at the end of the narrow gorge. They'd found this spot years ago, when they were partners, before Grant had betrayed him. Two of Bierdan's men rode through the opening with weapons drawn.

"Tell your men to put their guns away, Gordon. There's no point in any more dying over my cattle. We'll kill if needed, but it doesn't have to be that way."

"The hell it don't, Taylor," Gordon yelled. He reached over and drew his rifle from its scabbard. He didn't fire, but raced toward the opening at the other end of the gulley.

"Don't shoot. Bierdan is mine," Grant told his men and raced to his horse. He knew the lowland valley twisted and turned, which would slow Bierdan's escape. It was an easy trail down the back side for Grant. Only a few minutes and he'd meet up with the man who'd tried to gamble away their ranch years ago.

They'd been partners, grown the ranch into a success in only a few years. But Gordon's love of liquor and cards proved too much. He'd tried to put up his half of the ranch on a poker bet. One of the ranch hands overheard the bet and notified Grant, who sat with some other men at another table.

A few minutes later Gordon had been knocked out, dragged from the saloon, and thrown over his horse. Grant had known the bet wouldn't hold up in court due to a creative legal clause in the contract requiring both signatures for any transfer of land, but he'd been furious with his partner—felt he'd been deceived.

The next day Grant made Gordon an offer to buy his half, and the man had accepted. It was a fair offer, but as the years passed, Bierdan had convinced himself that Grant had stolen the property from him. No one else had seen it that way. Gordon's bitterness had increased and now it had come down to the simple truth that one would survive this day and one wouldn't.

Grant made it down the slope, dismounted, setup behind a large boulder, and waited. He saw Bierdan approach and leveled his rifle. "Stop, Gordon. I don't want to shoot you, but I will if you don't pull up."

"Not this time." Rifle in hand, Gordon reined in his horse, settled in the saddle, and pulled the trigger. "It's you or me today. I won't walk away again." He fired once more before dropping off his horse to hide behind a rock outcropping.

Grant moved around the boulder to get a better view. The last shot had ricocheted, grazing his left arm. "Give up, Gordon. You've got no chance of getting away and neither do your men. No reason for you to die."

"Go to hell, Taylor," Gordon shouted and squeezed the trigger.

The shot missed but now Grant knew where the man was hiding. He made his way around another small boulder and climbed up. He was looking down at his adversary twenty feet away. His boot slipped on the loose rock alerting Gordon to his location. Another shot buzzed past Grant at the same time he aimed and pulled the trigger. The bullet hit Gordon in the chest, spraying blood across the rocks and dirt. The rifle dropped from his hands as his legs gave out and he slumped to the ground.

Grant knelt next to the man he'd known for over thirty years and held his head. "It didn't have to be this way," he whispered.

Gordon's life beat out of him but he'd heard his old partner. "Sure it did." He coughed blood and spit. "At least I got one of them MacLaren men," he choked out. His eyes rolled back and his breath ceased.

******

"Doc says you've got to try to get something down, Drew. Now stop fighting me," Tess snapped.

"Leave me alone. I don't know how else to say it. I'm not hungry and I don't want you around," Drew snarled. She was trying to help but he didn't want to deal with this, with anything. He lay on his side, unable to move his legs, paralyzed.

"Well, that's too bad. You haven't put anything in your stomach since yesterday and

217

I'm not leaving until you try." Tess held her ground. "Of course, if you don't want me in here, I can always get Eleanor or your brothers to help out," she threatened.

He lowered his head to the pillow in defeat. "Fine. What is it?"

"Just broth. It won't kill you and it may take the edge off your foul mood." She smiled at his disgusted look. *He has to walk again,* she thought as she tried to help him turn just enough to make it easier to swallow.

The door opened and Amanda walked in as Drew finished the last drop. He did feel better, but he wouldn't let Tess know. She didn't need to get any closer to him. No one did. This was his problem and he'd figure out a way to handle it. Alone.

"Amanda, are they back?" Tess had checked several times out the window.

"They're riding up now with the cattle." Amanda's smile underscored the relief she felt. Grant was in the lead, with Will and Jamie not far behind. They were safe. "I'm going out to meet them."

"I'll be there in a minute," Tess called after her, but Amanda was already out the door.

Amanda walked out front just as her father and Jamie dismounted.

"Where's Will?" She looked around, but couldn't see him.

"He changed his mind about riding in with us. Said he needed some space and took off," Jamie replied in a disgusted tone. "How's Drew?"

218

"Good. Tess just finished getting him to swallow some broth, so he's awake."

"I'll be right in as soon as I take care of Rebel." He turned his horse toward the barn.

"What happened?" It didn't take Grant long to explain, including Gordon's confession to shooting Drew.

"Will took it hard. Felt the shot was meant for him. Seems that boy just goes from dealing with one tragedy to another." Grant hugged his daughter and walked into the house.

Amanda stood on the bottom step, worrying her bottom lip before making her decision. She didn't look back but walked straight to the barn. A few minutes later she rode out to find Will.

Chapter Twenty-Three

It was getting dark, but she kept riding, determined to find him. Will didn't need to be alone just now, and neither did she. He'd mentioned a couple of times about the views along the eastern boundary, how peaceful it was, and how it reminded him of the mountains around Fire Mountain. Jamie talked about going back with Drew and she knew Will would go with them. They'd ride out as quickly as they'd arrived and never look back. Somehow, though, Amanda knew life would never be the same for her or Tess.

A branch of the Grundy River ran along the property line. It was shallow enough to freeze most winters, but that was still a few months away. The sound of running water dancing over rocks was constant. It sounded the same as it had in her childhood, and when she had returned from her time in the East. Like life, the river just kept flowing.

She turned Angel toward the sound and found Justice. She reined in next to Will's horse and dropped to the ground. It was almost dark and she knew she should find Will and head home. That's when she saw him. He sat on the ground by the stream, knees bent, his arms draped over them, head down, and his hat pitched forward.

Amanda made her way across the fallen leaves and dried brush, trying not to disturb him. She was within a few feet when he looked up. His eyes were moist and Amanda realized she'd intruded at the worst possible time. She wanted to turn and run, but their eyes locked and after a moment he held out a hand to her.

They sat inches apart without saying a word. Will continued to hold her hand, at times giving it a slight squeeze and other times almost letting go. She wanted to tell him it was all right—all right to feel sorrow and all right to hold her hand—but she remained silent, not wanting to break the silence. Without warning he pulled her closer and put his arm around her, hugging Amanda to him. She dropped her head to his shoulder and nestled into his side.

Will had come here to mourn. Mourn his wife, the lost years, and most of all the vengeance that had paralyzed his brother. He knew about vengeance. Had thought it was a righteous feeling and had used it to justify his actions when tracking down his wife's killers. But now he saw how vengeance had been used against the wrong man. He knew it should be him at the house with useless legs and an uncertain future, not Drew. Not his twin who'd always been the peacemaker, the one to bring people together, not tear them apart.

And what would he do about his feelings for Amanda? Will had come to accept he'd fallen in love with this beautiful woman. But her life was here, on the family ranch, and his

221

was in Fire Mountain. Both were from ranching families, and both had their history in separate lands. He looked down at her and kissed the top of her head. She sighed and snuggled closer.

Amanda wondered if this was what love felt like. Strong arms, a comfortable silence, a feeling of peace. She didn't want it to end and tried to hold the moment in her heart, memorize it.

Tendrils of black hair had fallen across her face. Will reached around and tucked the strands behind her ear, then let his fingers trail down her cheek. When she looked up to him a tentative smile curved her lips. He cupped her cheek and brought his mouth down on hers for a whisper-soft kiss. It was meant to be short, just a brief touch, but once the bond was made neither seemed willing to break free.

Amanda's hand trailed up his arm to rest on his shoulder. She pulled him closer as he tightened his hold around her. The kiss continued, deepened, until her lips parted. Will knew they should stop, but he couldn't seem to pull away. It had been so long since he'd felt anything for another woman. He wasn't ready to let this feeling go, at least not yet. Reason warred with passion. If she made any attempt to stop, Will knew he would, but she seemed as lost in their shared hunger as he.

One hand moved up until it cupped her breast. He could feel her taut nipples through the fabric of her dress and thin chemise.

"I want you, Amanda, but we can't do this. I can't be your first, then leave for home. I'd never do that to you," he whispered as his lips hovered inches away.

The loss of his touch was almost painful, but she pulled back and looked up to see passion in his eyes, and something else. Could he have the same feelings for her that she had for him? "It's all right, Will. I..." but she couldn't finish—couldn't get the words out. Amanda took a deep, ragged breath, and tried to continue. "I'm not..." again words failed her.

The grief in her eyes tore at Will until what she kept trying to say made sense. She'd been with another man. This was not her first time.

"Tell me, Amanda," was all he said and pulled her closer. Minutes passed before she began to talk of her past. Her words were tentative at first, then began to flow. The pain and guilt came through in her halting speech and uneven voice. The fiancé she had met during school in the East. She'd thought she loved him. They were to marry in a few months, he'd told her. They didn't need to wait for the vows to consummate their love. She'd consented. Two weeks later he'd broken the engagement and within weeks married another young woman whom he said was more socially acceptable then a girl from the West. Amanda had been devastated. She'd

223

never told her parents and had only confided in one other person—Tessa.

The fury Will felt surprised him. He wanted to jump on Justice, ride cross-country, find the bastard, and ... and do what? Create another set of events he'd have to live with? No. What he wanted was right here in his arms. That was the reality he needed to face.

Amanda sat in silence and considered her next words. She looked up to stare into beautiful hazel eyes. "I want you to make love to me, Will. There'll be no promises, as I know you'd not be able to keep them. My life is here and yours is in Arizona. But we'll always have this to remember." She leaned up and kissed him lightly, letting her lips brush over his. Will's protest died. He stood and walked over to Justice, pulled the blanket roll from his saddle and carried it to a grassy area by the creek. He spread it out, then walked back to Amanda and held out his hand. There was no hesitancy in her grasp.

When they reached the blanket he turned her facing away from him and with slow movements unbuttoned her dress and let it fall to the ground. He drew her close and undid the pins in her hair, letting it fall down her back. Her black tresses were longer than he'd imagined, reaching to her waist. He draped them over her shoulder to place kisses along her neck as he gently lowered her chemise to her waist. His hand moved up to caress a breast, then moved to the other one. She turned in his arms and pulled his head down for another long, languid kiss. They dropped as one to the blanket and Amanda worked to release the buttons of his shirt, then shoved it off both shoulders to admire his solid, muscled chest.

Inch by inch he lowered her to the ground and his mouth claimed her breasts, first one, then the other. His hand moved up her legs, higher and higher, then stopped. Will took a deep, steadying breath and looked into Amanda's eyes for one final confirmation.

"Yes," was all she said before he continued and they gave each other what they both wanted.

******

They stayed by the creek long into the night as they made love twice more. Each time she began to pull away he reached for her. He didn't think he'd ever get enough of Amanda.

It was past midnight when they rode into the barn. The house was still lit but there was no sound coming through the boarded windows. Although the glass and destruction had been cleaned, it would take time for new windows to arrive and a new front door to be built.

Will helped Amanda down and drew her to him. He didn't want to let her go, not tonight, not ever. He had to find a way to work this out, convince her to come with him to Fire Mountain. Will dipped his head as she wrapped her arms around his neck for one last kiss before they left the privacy of the barn.

Will grabbed Angel's reins from Amanda. "I'll get the horses. You go ahead into the house. It's been a long day. We'll talk in the morning."

"Will, I..."

"We'll talk tomorrow."

She trudged to the house, up the steps, and closed the damaged front door—a reminder of all that had happened over the last two days. Light shown under Drew's door and she wondered if Tess might still be up, keeping him company. She turned the knob and peered in to see her sister rocking in a chair near the bed, eyes fixed on their injured friend.

"Tess?"

"Oh, Amanda. You're back. I wondered if you'd come home and already gone to bed." A weary yawn escaped Tess as she pushed herself from the chair. "He's resting again, which is good. When Drew's awake he's ornery, and when he sleeps he moans or sometimes calls out. I don't know if it's the laudanum or dreams, but it wakes him up most times. Doc is supposed be here in the morning to check on him."

"How does he seem?" Will's deep voice interrupted their whispered conversation. He walked to the bed and peered down at his identical twin who laid on his side, an arm outside of the covers. Drew had a birthmark on his right arm. It was one of the few ways to tell them apart.

"Angry, refuses to accept his legs won't work. Talks as if he'll be back on a horse in a few days," Tess replied. "Grant sent word to Louis Dunnigan about the shooting. Told him not to expect Drew anytime soon."

"What about pain?" Will asked.

"What the hell do you think? Hurts like hell," was Drew's response. He'd woken up to the sound of voices and tried with little success to roll to his back.

"You may not want to do that, Drew. The bullet wound..." Tess began but was interrupted.

"I know about the hole in my back, Tess. Can't feel the damn thing anyway," he grumbled and settled onto his left side.

"You need anything?" Will asked.

"Yea, to get out of this bed—on my own. That's all I need." Drew closed his eyes as the full impact of the injury hit him again. It was the same each time he woke up—curiosity as to why he was in bed and then recognition that he was injured, paralyzed. He might not accept that his legs may never work again, but at least he was beyond denying his current, sorry state. The despair he felt was overwhelming.

Will walked to the far side of the bed so he could get a better look at Drew's face. "Not going to happen tonight, but I know you and our family. If there's any chance at all for you to use those ugly legs of yours, we'll all be on your tail until you're sick of us or chase us away. On those two legs. Tomorrow we'll get you shaved. Uh, you need help with anything before I get comfortable?" Will glanced at the women but knew they grasped his meaning.

"No, got that covered. Grant helped me a few hours ago and I'm fine now."

"Well, I'm not going anywhere. Just going to sleep in the rocking chair there, so let me know if you need anything."

Drew didn't respond. He'd already drifted back to sleep.

"I'll stay here tonight, Tess. Get some rest. You've earned it," Will lowered himself into the chair.

"He's no bother, Will. I want to help him any way I can. Call me if you need anything." Tess took one more look at the man in the bed. She'd never been close to another man besides her father, Grant, and Jake. She'd never had a beau or been courted. Her shy nature and indifference kept most men away, but Drew was different. She wanted to be around him, get to know him, just not under these circumstances.

"Goodnight, Will. Try to get some rest," Amanda's eyes locked with Will's as she closed the door behind Tess and her.

Now it's you and me, brother, Will thought as he pushed back into the chair and began a slow, steady rocking motion. They'd been inseparable for years. Then they had allowed Cord McAllister to enter their group and the three had formed a bond that still remained. Will closed his eyes and wondered if Cord had quit his sheriff job in New Mexico and moved to Fire Mountain. He needed to get a message to him and the family. Let them all know what had happened. Those were his last thoughts before he drifted off to sleep.

Chapter Twenty-Four

Three days passed. The doctor came and left twice, the last time telling them no more laudanum. Drew couldn't feel the pain anyway and it just made talking with him more difficult.

It frustrated Will and Jamie to watch Drew lay there, day after day, trying to accept the situation and the possible long-term implications. The three had talked at length, twice. Each time Drew had adamantly refused to return to the ranch. Said he'd be no use to them if he couldn't walk or ride a horse. No, he'd insisted, he was not returning to Fire Mountain until he could ranch again.

Will and Amanda had only been able to find limited time together since their interlude at the stream. A few minutes in the kitchen before the day started, late in the barn when everyone else had turned in—but these had been only minutes, not enough for either of them. Will knew they had to talk.

Jamie decided to leave for home the next day. His and Torie's baby was due anytime, and he wanted to be there for her. He'd be back to help bring Drew home when his brother came to his senses. That meant Will's time in Cold Creek was short and he wanted to get his feelings out, convince Amanda that she was needed, beside him, in Fire Mountain.

Will had ridden out with Jake and several of the boys that morning to check the herd, make sure there weren't any more missing. Both knew the problem had been taken care of, but it felt good to be back on a horse after three days of sitting by Drew's bed, watching his labored breathing. He'd pull Amanda aside when he got back. They had to have that talk.

It was late afternoon when the group rode back to the ranch. Will unsaddled Justice, put away the tack, and finished grooming his horse. He'd just walked up the front steps when the door opened and a man he'd never seen before walked out.

The man took one look at him and stopped. His assessment was complete in five seconds. "Well, you must be Drew's twin brother. Will, correct?" He extended his hand, which Will accepted.

"Yes, sir. Will MacLaren. And you are?"

"Louis Dunnigan. I own the company where Drew works. Got word of the shooting and decided it best to come out here and let your brother know it makes no difference to me if he walks or not. His job is secure and I want him back in Denver." Dunnigan turned to glance back into the house as he talked. The man knew what he wanted, and right now that was Drew, back in Denver.

"Goodbye, Mrs. Taylor, Mr. Taylor. Thank you so much for taking such good care of Drew for us," a woman's voice came from inside the home. "I'll speak with Father, but I'm confident Drew will be going back to

Denver with us when we leave tomorrow." The voice walked out of the house and Will saw it was attached to a young woman about Amanda's age. She wore what he could only describe as the most expensive day dress he'd ever seen. Her brown hair was hidden under a small-brimmed hat that was a good eight inches high and adorned with feathers. In one hand she carried a parasol and in the other a small, leather purse.

"Ah, Patricia. I'd like you to meet Drew's brother, Will MacLaren. Will, my daughter, Patricia. She insisted on coming along to check on her fiancé." Dunnigan completed the introductions and turned to answer a question from Grant.

"Fiancé?" Will's puzzled expression wasn't lost on Patricia.

"Why, yes, Mr. MacLaren. Did he not tell you we are betrothed?" Patricia batted her eyes so fast Will wondered if she might have some type of affliction.

"It's Will, and no ma'am, Drew never mentioned anything about a fiancée."

"Oh, well, you know how men are about such things."

"No, ma'am, I don't, but I aim to find out. Excuse me, Miss Dunnigan. I need to speak with my brother. It's been, um, a pleasure." Will made a slight bow and walked past Patricia to head straight for Drew's room. Jamie was already there when Will pushed through the door.

"What's going on? There's a lady out front saying she's your fiancée, and Louis Dunnigan is saying he's taking you back to Denver. That right, Drew?" Will's voice was hard, almost angry at the way things were going.

"Yea, well, Patricia is a little pushy on the matter. She's been telling people we're getting married for months. Fact is, I haven't asked the lady and hadn't planned to, but now, well, it may be for the best." Jamie took one side. Will took the other, and they lifted Drew to a sitting position. Laying on his side was easy but made breathing hard.

"For the best? What's that supposed to mean?" Will didn't like the direction of this conversation.

"Mr. Dunnigan wants me back in Denver. He's already bought a house in town and has men setting it up so I can get around in a wheelchair. Got a chair already ordered." Drew grabbed a glass of water by the bed and took a long, slow swallow. "It's for the best, Will. I can work there, be useful. He wants me to marry his daughter, and well, maybe I'll just do that, too." He sounded defensive, resigned.

"That's bull, Drew, and you know it. You don't want to live in Denver any more than I do. Your life is with us, on the ranch." Will ran a hand through his auburn colored hair. "You were going to quit anyway, if I remember right."

Drew took a deep breath. No, he didn't want to return to the city and his old job, but

233

what choice did he have? For a few brief moments, before the shooting, he'd imagined what life would be like with Tess. They were much alike. She loved books and quiet time, was soft-spoken, and dreamed of breeding the best horses in Colorado, the same as Drew and Will. That's a woman he could fall for, live the rest of his life with. But he had nothing to offer her now. Hell, he didn't know if he could even have children. Patricia wasn't interested in that, and truth be told, he couldn't imagine having them with her. At least he knew he could make a good living in Denver doing legal work. Dunnigan wanted to make him a partner. That meant that one day he'd be a very wealthy man.

"Well, things change, Will, and that means I need to rethink my future. I've made up my mind. I'll go back with them tomorrow and learn to live with these useless legs. Right now it's the best I can do." His voice was firm, heart-breaking in its finality.

"But the doctor said it could be temporary. What if it is? What if the feeling returns and you walk again? You gonna be satisfied in Denver then?" Jamie had stayed quiet, listening to the twins hash out Drew's future. He wanted to slam a fist into the wall, tell Drew it was crap that he wouldn't return to the ranch and surround himself with people who loved him and would always be there for him. But who was he to bring it up? He'd done much the same thing years before. In time, it had all worked out for Jamie. Maybe it would for Drew, also.

"If feeling returns and I can walk again? I guess we'll have to wait and see, but in the meantime, I plan to be useful and not lay in a damn bed all day wishing things were different."

"And Miss Dunnigan? You plan to jump into a marriage of convenience with someone you don't love?" Will still couldn't believe Drew's future was playing out this way.

"Not right away. I'll give it time, decide if she's who I want." But he already knew Patricia would never be the woman he wanted. Tess's face flashed in his mind, but he shook it off. There was no need to dwell on what was no longer possible. "Dunnigan made it clear my job doesn't ride on me marrying his daughter, but he'd like for that to happen. Right now I need to concentrate on walking again and doing work I feel good about."

"You're sure about this?" Jamie asked.

"Sure as anything," Drew's voice was flat, reconciled to an uncertain future.

"Will, I'm going to wait for Dunnigan to come for Drew tomorrow, then I'll ride for home. You coming with me?" Jamie wanted his brother home—all the family did.

"Yea, I'll be ready when you are." There was no joy in Will's voice. Drew was going back to Denver and he knew he'd have a heck of a battle getting Amanda to follow him to Fire Mountain. He needed to talk with her and see if they had any chance of a future together.

******

Dinner was somber. Eleanor prepared a grand meal, knowing this might be the last time they'd have Jamie, Will, and Drew at their table. She felt like they were losing family, not men they'd only known a brief time. The brothers carried Drew out and set him up in a tall chair, a pillow on each side for support.

Drew had his first normal meal since the shooting, and it tasted good—steak, mashed potatoes, corn, biscuits, and berry pie. He ate a small amount of everything, then pushed back from the table to stand before his brain kicked in to remind him that standing wasn't possible, at least tonight.

"Dunnigan said he and his daughter would be here early in the morning to get you, Drew. They've got a special carriage for the ride to the train station in Great Valley. Looks like you'll be in Denver tomorrow night," Grant said. He'd never be able to repay the MacLaren's for their help. If only things could've turned out different for Drew.

"Thanks, Mr. Taylor. I appreciate everything you and your family have done for me." Drew's voice was strained.

"No need to thank us. It's us who are grateful to you and your brothers."

"I'll help clear the table, Mother," Amanda started to push away from the table.

Will spoke up. "Amanda, I wondered if maybe you'd be free to take a walk?" Heads snapped in his direction but he ignored them and focused his gaze on the beautiful woman sitting next to him.

"Well, yes, Will. I'd like that, if it's okay with Mother."

"Of course, Amanda, you go with Will. Tess can help me."

The pair made their way into the cool night air. It was fall. It wouldn't be long before they got their first snow. Chores would take longer but everyone was used to the change in seasons. They walked around the barn toward the back corrals and he grabbed her hand in his. She wondered if she'd ever see Will again after tomorrow. Her chest tightened at the thought that the answer could be no.

When the house was out of sight, Will pulled her to him and captured her lips with his. Her arms circled his neck to draw his face down. He moved his lips over her face to her eyes, then let them trail down her neck to the top of her blouse, before taking her lips again. He wanted more, much more, but now wasn't the time. They needed to talk. Decide if they had a future.

Will pulled back to look into her deep blue eyes. They were damp, but no tears fell. "I love you, Amanda. Marry me. Come home to Fire Mountain and build a life with me," Will said before he lost his nerve.

She heard the words, but her mind took a moment to process their meaning. He loved

237

her and wanted to marry her. He was offering everything she wanted—him—but in Arizona, not Colorado. She had a life here, a ranch to help run, and her family. It would mean giving up everything for a man she'd known for only a few weeks.

Will watched her eyes widen at his declaration, but she remained silent. He had no idea as to what she was thinking. Maybe she didn't love him. Perhaps he'd misjudged her feelings towards him. "Amanda, did you hear me?" he asked when he could no longer stand the uncertainty.

"Yes, Will, I heard you. I just, well, don't know what to say."

"How about you love me. That would be a good start."

She smiled as she looked into his eyes. "I do love you, Will. More than you know. And I'd marry you, tonight if we could," she began.

"That's good for me. I'll ride to town now and get the preacher," he said before she could utter the "but" he knew for certain was coming.

"Except, how do I leave the ranch, the family, everything, for a life in a land I know nothing about?" She prayed he would have an answer that would sweep away her misgivings.

"You'd leave because we love each other and want to build a life, raise a family together."

"But I have responsibilities here. Father expects me to take over the ranch someday.

He and Mother count on me for so much more than you've seen. I can't just walk away, don't you see?" She wanted to go with him. She loved him. But she didn't see how it was possible.

"You wouldn't be leaving them alone, Amanda. They have Tessa and Joey, plus Jake and everyone else. Grant isn't old. He has a lot of years of ranching left."

"Oh, Will, I want to go with you. I love you. But I can't leave, not right now. Maybe sometime in the future." She paused to gather her thoughts. "I can't go with you, but you can stay. We could build a life here," she pleaded. The thought of Will leaving caused a crushing pain in her chest, but the thought of leaving the Taylor Ranch and her family triggered the same intense pain. Amanda felt caught between two equally imposing forces with nowhere to turn.

"I see. You love me but you won't consider a life with me unless I stay here, at your family's ranch, is that right?" Will's already scratchy voice had turned hard, much like it had been the first few times they'd spoken. Her heart sank. He wouldn't even consider it.

"Well, yes, that's what I'm saying. You haven't worked your ranch for years. Must you return now? Couldn't we stay here and let your other brothers take over for you?"

Will's face turned to stone. She hadn't seen him look this hard since the day he'd warned her not to follow him. He'd pushed her away then and he was doing the same now. "No, Amanda, I can't push my work on them any longer. I have responsibilities, also. They've pulled my share of the load for five years. I can't expect them to do it now that Hawley is dead."

So this was the end. There was no future for them.

"If that's your answer, then I guess it's best we head back to the house. Jamie and I have a long ride tomorrow and I want to check on Drew before I bed down." Will turned, but stopped when he heard Amanda's voice.

"Will, I do love you. I wish you could understand that I must stay here, with my family," Amanda said softly. The misery in her voice did nothing to make Will feel better about the outcome.

"It's all right. You have to make choices and so do I. I'd hoped you'd choose me."

Their walk to the house seemed to take forever. Amanda didn't know what else she could say to make him at least consider staying. Why did he insist she was the one who had to make all the changes, leave her family, and give up the life she knew?

Will grabbed her hand and turned Amanda to him as they approached the house. "If you change your mind, you know where to find me." He bent down for one last kiss before escorting her into the home she'd chosen.

Chapter Twenty-Five

"I guess we're ready," Louis Dunnigan said when Drew was in the elaborate carriage, Patricia settled beside him. The somber mood from the night before had continued into the morning. No one seemed happy about Drew's return to Denver, but it was his decision to make.

Amanda and Tess watched as Jamie and Will reined their horses up next to the carriage. They planned to escort Drew and the Dunnigans as far as they could before turning west, then south toward Fire Mountain. They'd all said their goodbyes. There was no more reason to wait.

"Grant, Eleanor, thanks again for everything," Drew called from the window.

"You just take care of yourself, son, and let us know how you're doing," Grant replied. Drew nodded his response. Grant turned to Jamie and Will. "And you two better stay in touch also. If you're ever up this way we expect a visit—no excuses."

"Yes, sir," both answered.

Dunnigan signaled to his driver to go. Jamie rode out front a few yards followed by Will. But a few minutes later, Will turned Justice around and pulled up in front of Amanda. "You remember what I said,

Amanda." That was all. He left on the journey home.

******

It was a slow trek by wagon to the train station in Great Valley where Will and Jamie would watch Drew board the train for Denver. From there, they'd ride in the other direction, to Arizona and the rest of their family.

Drew sat in the carriage and thought of a future without ranching. He'd never thought his life would turn out this way, but then he guessed no one ever thought their life would change to such a degree. Death, yes, but this, no. The hardest part was the knowledge that he'd need someone in the house or office who could help him with basic needs, at least until he could overcome the paralysis and walk again.

He rested his head against the back of the padded seat and closed his eyes. An image of Tess flashed through his mind. She was laughing. It was the day he'd helped her improve her aim. She'd worked for over an hour and had at last begun to hit the target. The pleasure in her eyes made him smile, even now, as he jostled back and forth in the carriage. She'd laughed when her last shot had hit the bucket at just the right spot and it had toppled over, spilling the rocks inside.

The next image was the shock on her face when Patricia had introduced herself as his fiancée. Tess had recovered well. That's when it had dawned on him that she might feel more for him than she'd let on, but nothing he could say would change the fact that Tess believed there was another woman in his life. It was for the best, Drew reasoned. Without the use of his legs he had nothing to offer a young ranch-woman who dreamed of breeding horses. No, his future lay in the city.

The sound of the railroad pulled Drew from his thoughts of Tess. They'd arrived in Great Valley. It was time to move on with his life and leave the old one behind.

With help from Will and Jamie, Drew boarded the train and settled into one of Dunnigan's two luxurious private cars. The car had everything they'd need for the trip, plus it offered privacy from the other passengers. He watched his brothers scan the interior. He'd never thought about it, as he'd ridden in the cars numerous times, but it was much more grand than most people realized. The problem was, it wasn't where he wanted to be, and it wasn't going home.

"You let us know how you're doing. Don't make us travel to Denver to find out," Jamie chided him as he gave him as close of a hug as they could manage. "You know Aunt Alicia's going to want to come for a visit, so you might as well plan on it now."

"Yea, I know. She's welcome any time. All of you are welcome any time." Drew's voice was thick with emotion. Even though he'd planned to return to Denver for a short while, he'd never expected it to be permanent.

"I'm still not happy with this decision," Will said as he hugged his twin and stood. "You send a message as soon as you come to your senses and I'll come get you. You understand?" His eyes narrowed at his brother and the silent message he sent wasn't lost on Drew.

"I understand, and I'll be in touch. But don't worry about me. I'll beat this thing and be walking before you know it." Drew smiled but it didn't reach his eyes.

"Train's ready to leave, gentlemen. I wish we'd met under different circumstances, but be assured, your brother is in good hands." Louis Dunnigan walked the brothers to the door and watched them step to the platform. "We'll keep you posted on his progress. He'll get the best doctors and treatment possible. You've got my word on it."

"Mr. Dunnigan, we'll hold you to that," Will shouted as the train began to pull away.

The brothers watched in silence as the train moved farther east and out of sight. "Come on, Will. Time to get you home," Jamie said and the two mounted up for the trip to Fire Mountain.

******

"Did you know he had a fiancée, Amanda?" Tess asked later that day as the two of them set the table for supper. She'd been more quiet than usual, plagued by her constant thoughts of Drew.

244

"No, but I'm not sure Drew realized he had a fiancée, either. Something just doesn't quite fit."

"He told me they weren't engaged but said Patricia had talked about it for months. Perhaps it's just her way. Guess it doesn't matter. I'll never see him again, anyway," the sad tone got Amanda's attention.

"Do you love him, Tess?"

"No, at least I don't believe so," Tess lied. "But I do care about him much more than I realized. If only he could've stayed here, on the ranch, maybe..." but she didn't finish, just shook her head and finished with the table, then looked up at Amanda. "What happened with you and Will?"

"What happened? I'm not sure I know what you mean." Amanda wasn't interested in a discussion about Will, at least not yet. She was still trying to reconcile herself to the fact that he was gone and she'd refused to go with him.

"I may not have any experience with men, but I'm not blind. You have feelings for him, and it's obvious he cares for you. What was it Will said to you when he left? Something about 'remember what I said?'"

"It doesn't matter, Tess. Truth is, I don't want to think about Will, or Drew, or any of the MacLarens. Let's just be glad they were here to help when we needed it and they're all alive." Amanda felt the weight of her decision like a vice around her chest. Had she made a mistake, letting him ride off without her?

Well, it was too late now. He was gone and she'd just have to live with her decision.

******

"Eleanor, you have any idea what's going on with Amanda?" Grant asked.

She glanced up at her husband and a slight smile tugged at the corners of her mouth. "You don't know, dear?" Eleanor tightened her grip on his hand. They'd gotten into the habit of taking a stroll each night while on their trip and realized how much they enjoyed the quiet time outside together.

"Know what?" Grant's voice filled with frustration. He'd been watching his oldest daughter sink deeper into a black mood while Eleanor seemed to know what had triggered it.

"She's in love, Grant."

"Amanda, in love? With who?"

"Why, I think it's obvious. Will MacLaren. And from what I could tell, he feels the same for her." Eleanor enjoyed the confusion on her husband's face.

"I'll be damned," was all Grant could say as he absorbed the news. "Well then, why didn't anyone say anything to us? And why is she here and he in Arizona?"

"Oh, Grant, think about it. Our ranch is here and you've always told her how much you count on her to take it over some day. She loves you, would do anything you asked. What do you think she would have told Will?"

"You mean the boy asked her to marry him?"

"I don't know if he asked her or not, but I do know our daughter and her fierce loyalty. She would have turned him down if it meant leaving the ranch."

Grant mulled this over for a spell and thought back to when he had asked Eleanor to marry him and leave her life in England for the unknown of Colorado. It had been a hard decision for her. She would be giving up everything to be with him. But she'd done it, and her parents had gone along with her decision. How could he do any less for their daughter?

"What do you think we should do about this situation? She's not much good here if her heart's not in it, and I'll wager the same thing's going on with that boy."

"I think we should just ask. We've always been honest with each other, and her. I see no reason to change now."

"All right, that's what we'll do. Tomorrow at breakfast. I don't want to go through another day watching that sad face of hers. But I'll tell you, Eleanor, I won't look forward to losing her. We can cope with the ranch. I just know my heart's going to have a hard time adjusting," Grant said as he squeezed his wife's hand.

******

"Place is looking great, Niall. You and Jamie have done a lot of work since I was last home, and it shows," Will said to his oldest brother. It had been almost a month since he'd left Colorado, his brother, and Amanda. They'd gotten a couple of messages from Drew. He was doing better, even though feeling had not returned to his legs. But there'd been no word from Cold Creek. Not that he'd expected any. She'd been firm in her rejection, and even though he'd understood her reasons, it had hurt just the same.

"Got to be honest, Will. Having you back has made a big difference. I've never seen a man work as hard as you have the last few weeks. Almost like you're trying to push something or someone out of your mind." Niall shot a quick glance at his brother. He knew something still plagued Will, and with Hawley dead, a woman was all Niall figured it could be.

"She turned me down, Niall. It's over and that's all I'm going to say." Will stooped to grab another rail for the fence repair they'd worked on for three days.

"Fair enough," Niall replied as he grabbed the other end of the rail.

"What's going on with Trent? Haven't seen him but twice since I've been back. Thought with Kate here he'd be a fixture at this place."

"Ah, Trent's in love."

"In love? With who?" Will was stunned. They'd known Trent since Will was seven and Niall was fifteen. He'd been a U.S. Marshal at

248

that time and had helped the boys make the trek from Ohio to Arizona after raiders murdered their parents. His daughter, Kate, had married Niall several years ago. Trent had retired from the Marshal Service and now owned a ranch that shared their property line for a few miles. He was close with all four of the MacLaren brothers.

"Joanne Babbitt." Niall smiled. Trent had been widowed years ago, it was time he connected with a good woman, and Joanne Babbitt was a very good woman. She'd been his housekeeper for over five years. Niall was surprised it had taken Trent so long to see her for what she was—a beautiful, mature woman who'd be devoted to him.

"Well I'll be damned. Mrs. Babbitt. Makes sense, though, and he couldn't ask for a better woman."

"The ceremony is a week from Saturday. Aunt Alicia insisted everyone come to our place after the church service. Hope you're up for a whole troop of visitors 'cause she's planned one heck of a shindig," Niall laughed. Aunt Alicia, his wife, Kate, and Jamie's wife, Torie, had been told of the betrothal only a few days ago, but word was already out and so far most of the town planned to attend.

"Sounds fine to me. It'll give me a chance to see people I haven't had a chance to visit yet." *And get my mind off Amanda*, he hoped.

"I'm finished. Let's head in and get supper before Jamie and the kids devour it all," Niall said as he packed up their tools.

"Not tonight. I'm headed over to Cord and June's for supper, but I'll see you at breakfast first thing in the morning." Will had only seen the McAllister's a few times since his return. Between the work at the ranch and Cord's new job as Sam Browning's deputy, it had been hard to work in the time. But at least he no longer had to travel to New Mexico to see them.

Chapter Twenty-Six

"So what are you asking, Father? I'm not sure I understand," a confused Amanda asked, and stole a look at her Mother.

"I'm asking if you have a beau, someone you want to spend time with." He'd tried to find the right words to ask about Will, but he'd apparently failed.

"What your Father is asking, dear, is whether you're in love with Will MacLaren," Eleanor chimed in as she took another small bite of her eggs.

"Will MacLaren?" Amanda choked out.

"Yes, Will MacLaren. A simple yes or no will be fine, dear."

"Well..." Amanda started, only to be interrupted by her father.

"Do you love him or not, Amanda?"

She'd never lied to her parents and she saw no point in it now. "Yes, Father. I do love Will."

"And does he love you?"

"Yes, Father, he says he does."

At least now they knew what had had their daughter brooding for weeks. "But he didn't ask you to marry him?" Eleanor asked.

"Yes, Mother, he asked me but I turned him down. He expected me to live on his ranch in Arizona and I just couldn't do that—

not with our ranch here." Amanda was struck by a sudden awareness. Her mother must have gone through the same painful decision process, but had chosen a different path than Amanda had.

The room fell silent. Grant and Eleanor knew their next words had to be spoken with care. They loved Amanda, but knew she'd be miserable staying in Colorado out of a sense of duty when her heart insisted she leave for Arizona to build a life with the man she loved.

Grant cleared his throat. "Amanda, you know how much you mean to your Mother and me. We love you without reservation and that won't change, no matter where you choose to live. As important as this ranch is to us, your happiness means a great deal more. If you love Will, and he loves you, then don't let the ranch come between you and that love. The ranch will be here, and so will we. We'll always be here for you." He reached over to set his large, rough hand atop his daughter's and smiled.

Amanda looked at their joined hands then up to her mother's tear filled eyes. Eleanor could only nod in agreement and smile at her daughter.

Tess sat stone still during the entire conversation. She'd suspected her sister had deep feelings for Will, but hadn't pushed. Now she was both elated that Grant and Eleanor had given their blessing, and sad to know their time together was so short. Amanda would leave for the MacLaren ranch in

Arizona soon, Tess was sure of it. It would be lonely without her.

"Amanda, you know I'm happy for you and Will, but I will miss you a great deal," Tess leaned across her chair to hug her sister.

"Joey, aren't you going to say anything?" Eleanor asked.

"Ah, I knew they were sweet on each other all along," he replied, but smiled at Amanda. Truth was, he'd miss her, but there was no chance he'd get all mushy about it.

******

"One more load of chairs and that should do it," Will called to his Aunt Alicia. Trent and Joanne's wedding was at noon. Afterwards, everyone would ride back to the MacLaren ranch for the reception. They figured a couple hundred people would come—not the whole town, but a fair number. "Anything else before I clean up?"

"No, Will, that should do it. The food's made and the house is ready. You go ahead and change. I'll ask Niall to get the wagon."

******

The ceremony was beautiful. Trent was resplendent in his black dress coat and slacks with a deep green brocade vest, black hat, and shiny boots. Joanne wore a light shade of green. Her nineteen-year-old daughter, Alma, and fifteen-year-old son, Tommy, beamed as their mother took her vows. Their father had walked out on the family almost six years before and Trent had taken them in, given them chores and a home, but most important, acceptance.

Everyone went back to the MacLaren ranch for the festivities, enjoying the band and eating until they couldn't take one more bite. The bar was open. Per Alicia's strict instructions it offered two items—punch and water. Of course, no one objected if the men wanted to add a little more flavor to their punch.

Will looked around at the remaining guests. Many had left but a good number had stayed to talk and dance. It had been a good day. He was glad his friend, Cord McAllister, had taken the job with Sam. Sam was a good man and would treat Cord with respect. They'd been huddled for an hour on the front porch, talking of the recent string of horse thefts around the area. Rustling. That was one item Will didn't want to face again anytime soon, but ranching was a tough business and thieving was just another part of every rancher's life.

An image of Amanda drifted into his mind. Her head was thrown back and her long black hair fell in loose waves to her waist. Her deep blue eyes flashed as she laughed at something Will had said. They were at the stream, splashing water on their faces and dressing before the ride back to the Taylor ranch. His heart clenched at the memory and he swallowed the disappointment that haunted a little of each day. He'd move on, he knew it, but it would be a long time before he found anyone else who affected him like Amanda did.

******

"Well, Amanda, we're only a few miles out. Still want to go through with this plan of yours? Showing up without warning can create a heap of trouble, and disappointment," Grant said as he rode alongside his daughter. He and Eleanor had agreed she could travel to Fire Mountain but only if Grant rode with her. No sense taking a buggy. It would just slow them down, and if things didn't work out as Amanda hoped, horses would make for a faster retreat.

"Yes, this is still what I want to do. If he's changed his mind, well then, at least I'll know and can move on with my life." Amanda's stomach tightened at the thought that Will might not still love her, want to marry her. But somehow, she believed that once a MacLaren man fell in love, it would be until death.

It was dark when they rode up to the MacLaren house. The house was well lit and laughter wafted through the windows into the cool night air. A few horses and a couple of buggy's sat outside, evidence that they may have company. Well, she and her father couldn't turn back toward town now. It was late and both were exhausted.

Amanda dismounted and watched her father slide off of his horse. He was as agile now as he'd been when she was a girl. She'd miss his strength and unwavering support, but he was right, her life was here, with Will. If he still wanted her.

She tried to brush the dust off her split skirt and tucked loose strands of hair up into her hat. Amanda knew she must look a mess, but there was no help for it now. They were here. She took a deep breath to steady her nerves and started up the front steps, Grant right behind her. Laughter poured from the house, and for a brief instant she wanted to turn and run.

"It's okay, Amanda. Go ahead and knock," Grant said from his spot next to her. She nodded, lifted her hand, and knocked three times on the wood door.

"I'll get it," someone said from inside, but it wasn't a voice Amanda recognized. The door opened and a girl of about twelve or thirteen stared up at her. "Hello. I'm Beth MacLaren. Are you here to see Trent and Joanne?" the girl asked.

Amanda's throat went dry and she froze. *What was I thinking coming here unannounced?*

"Are you all right?" Beth asked as she held the door open.

Amanda swallowed and nodded her head. "Yes, yes, I'm fine. I'm Amanda Taylor and this is my father, Grant Taylor. I've come to see Will—if he's at home." There, she'd said it. There would be no turning back now.

"Oh, he's here all right, along with most of the family who were at the wedding today. Come on in, I'll get him," Beth indicated that Amanda and Grant should wait inside. The word "wedding" had Amanda's heart racing and she wondered, only for a brief moment, if he'd changed his mind and

256

married another. But no, she simply wouldn't believe that.

Beth turned and walked the few feet to the living room entry. "Uncle Will, there's a lady here to see you." Conversation stopped and Will looked up from his discussion with Cord.

"A lady, huh?" Will's heart began to pound. Could it be? But he refused to believe she'd changed her mind. He walked across the room and turned toward the entry. His heart slammed into his chest. Amanda had come to him.

"Amanda..." was all he could get out as he walked towards her.

"Will, I know this is unannounced..." Her words trailed off as Will grabbed her by the waist and swung her around. She began to laugh as he set her on the floor before grabbing her face in both palms.

"You came," he said, then drew her face up for a long kiss before he pulled back to look at her once again. "Tell me you're here to stay, Amanda. Tell me you'll marry me."

Her smile was broad. "Yes, Will. I'll marry you and live here, at the ranch, if you still want me."

Will backed away, grabbed her hand, and pulled her toward the living room. "Everyone, this is Amanda Taylor, and she's just agreed to marry me."

The brief silence was broken when Jamie walked over to Amanda and gave her a hug. "Welcome to the family, Amanda. We're real glad to have you."

"Who's Amanda?" Kate whispered to her husband, Niall.

"I don't rightly know, but I guess we're all about to find out," he said and smiled at his wife. It has turned into a truly memorable day, Niall thought as he leaned over to place a kiss on Kate's cheek.

Epilogue

"Would you like to hold him, Amanda?" Torie turned toward her new sister-in-law and held out Caleb. He was the most beautiful baby Amanda had ever seen. He'd been born only days after Jamie had returned from the Taylor ranch in Colorado.

"What do you think, Mrs. MacLaren? Would you like about a dozen like him?" Will asked. He walked up beside her and wrapped a possessive arm around her waist.

"A dozen?" She laughed. "Not a dozen, but a couple of boys and girls would do just fine for me, Mr. MacLaren." Amanda smiled at her new husband. He wondered if he'd ever get over the way her smile seemed to knock the air from him.

They'd been married that morning and everyone was at the ranch to celebrate. They'd decided to hold the wedding in Fire Mountain after Grant and Eleanor had informed them they would bring the rest of their family as well as a wagon filled with Amanda's possessions.

"Four is good for me, too," Will said and bent down to kiss his wife on the tip of her nose. He looked back up at the mass of friends and family and thought of Emily. They'd shared a good life, if only for a brief time, and he would always love her. But Amanda was his life now and he knew they'd build a strong, devoted family, the way MacLarens always did.

The thought made his mind skip to Drew. He hadn't been able to make the wedding. A telegram from Louis Dunnigan had arrived two days earlier saying Drew was doing well but having trouble adjusting to his paralysis. It had been weeks since the shooting and feeling had still not returned below his waist. No one was giving up, but as time went on, they all knew Drew's chances of walking again were slipping away.

"I want to speak with Tess a minute, Will," Amanda said and handed Caleb back to Torie. Her sister had been more quiet than normal the past few days. Amanda suspected she knew why, but had been hesitant to say anything. But time was short. Her family was leaving to return to their Colorado ranch in the morning. This might be her only opportunity to speak to Tess in private.

She found her sitting in a swing on the porch, watching, but not participating, in the celebration. "Mind if I sit?" Amanda asked. They sat a while in comfortable silence before Amanda spoke.

"Why don't you go to Denver and check on him, Tess?"

"How did you know that's what I was thinking?"

"Well, let's see. I've known you for almost twenty years, we're sisters, and I'm about ninety-percent sure you love Drew."

Tess began to protest, but stopped. Amanda was right—she did love Drew. But he'd indicated no similar feelings for her. "He's never spoken of any feelings for me. What if it's one-sided and he sends me away?"

"You go as a friend, not as someone expecting anything from him. His focus is on walking and I'll bet he could use a friend, someone he knows wants nothing from him but to help. That's you, Tess, not Louis Dunnigan and not Patricia. Go to Denver, be his friend. You'll never know what could be until you take the chance." Amanda watched Tess absorb her words, then settled back against the swing.

When she looked up she saw a different expression on her sister's face—determination mixed with a calm acceptance. At that moment Amanda realized that Tess had made her choice.

Other books in the MacLarens of Fire Mountain series by Shirleen Davies

Tougher than the Rest

Niall MacLaren is determined to turn his ranch into the biggest cattle dynasty in the Arizona Territory. The widower will do whatever he must to obtain the political and financial support he needs, even marry a woman he does not love. Nothing will stand in his way.

Katherine is well-bred, educated, and seeks a life away from her cloistered existence in the East. Landing the teaching job in California provides her with the opportunity she seeks. Most importantly, and unlike many of her peers, she will not need a husband to achieve her goals.

When an accident brings them together, mutual desire takes root, threatening to dismantle their carefully laid plans and destroy their dreams. Can either of them afford to be distracted by the passion that unites them—especially when one of them may belong to another?

Faster than the Rest

Handsome, ruthless, young U.S. Marshal Jamie MacLaren had lost everything—his parents, his family connections, and his childhood sweetheart—but now he's back in Fire Mountain and ready for another chance. Just as he successfully reconnects with his family and starts to rebuild his life, he gets the unexpected and unwanted assignment of rescuing the woman who broke his heart.

Beautiful, wealthy Victoria Wicklin chose money and power over love, but is now fighting for her life—or is she? Who has she become in the seven years since she left Fire Mountain to take up her life in San Francisco? Is she really as innocent as she says?

Marshal MacLaren struggles to learn the truth and do his job, but the past and present lead him in different directions as his heart and brain wage battle. Is Victoria a victim or a villain? Is life offering him another chance, or just another heartbreak?

As Jamie and Victoria struggle to uncover past secrets and come to grips with their shared passion, another danger arises. A life-altering danger that is out of their control and threatens to destroy any chance for a shared future.

Stronger than the Rest

Dedicated, handsome, and smart, Drew MacLaren is the true scholar of the family but yearns to return to the family ranch in Fire Mountain. Read about his story in Book Four of the MacLarens of Fire Mountain.

About the Author

Shirleen Davies began her new series, MacLarens of Fire Mountain, with Tougher than the Rest, the story of the oldest brother, Niall MacLaren. During the day she provides consulting services to small and mid-sized businesses. But her real passion is writing emotionally charged stories of flawed people who find redemption through love and acceptance. She grew up in Southern California and now lives with her husband in a beautiful town in northern Arizona. Between them they are the proud parents of five grown sons.

Shirleen loves to hear from her readers.
Write to her at shirleen@shirleendavies.com
Visit her at www.shirleendavies.com
Check out her blog at
www.shirleendavies.com/blog.html

Thank you!

Made in the USA
Coppell, TX
27 July 2021